Off
in
Zimbabwe

AWP-7

Off in Zimbabwe

Stories by Rod Kessler

University of Missouri Press
Columbia, 1985

Library of Congress Cataloging in Publication Data

Kessler, Rod.
  Off in Zimbabwe.

  I. Title.
PS3561.E713034   1985   813'.54   84-19624
ISBN 0-8262-0470-8

Many of the stories in this collection were written or revised
while I was the George Bennett Memorial Fellow at Phillips
Exeter Academy in New Hampshire. I am grateful to the school
for providing me with a year for writing.

"Lieutenant" appeared in *Intro 13*
"An Infidelity" appeared in the *Greensboro Review*
"Mailman" appeared in *Cache Review*
"Benny and I" appeared in *Cottonwood Review*
"How to Touch a Bleeding Dog" appeared in *Mazagine*
"A Member of the Class" appeared in *Passages North*
"The Death of Rodney Snee" appeared in *Tellus 8*
"Another Thursday with the Meyerhoffs" appeared in *Midway
Review*
"Off in Zimbabwe" appeared in *Signal Fire*
"Carter" appeared in the *New Mexico Humanities Review*
"Victoria and Jerry" appeared in *The Pendulum*
"My Name Is Buddy" appeared in *Fiction 83*
"October Reeds" appeared in the *Apalachee Quarterly*

For Guri

The AWP Award Series in Short Fiction

This volume is the first-place winner of the sixth annual AWP Award Series in Short Fiction, sponsored by the Associated Writing Programs, an organization of over ninety colleges and universities with strong curricular commitments to the teaching of creative writing, headquartered at Old Dominion University, Norfolk, Virginia.

Each year a collection of outstanding short fiction is selected by a panel of distinguished fiction writers from among the many manuscripts submitted to the AWP Award Series competition. The University of Missouri Press is proud to be associated with the series and to present *Off in Zimbabwe* as this year's selection.

Contents

Lieutenant

Face it, she had said, *you were the lieutenant*. She had already moved most of her stuff out. *I'm tired of your pretenses.* My old lady—walking out. *I'm sick of your nonsense, your alligators. Face up to things*, she'd said. *Go see a shrink.* See a shrink.

Her breath always reminded me of raisins. Does Reese notice it now, sweet and heavy? Does he like it?

How long has it been now? Does it matter? No one interferes anymore.

*   *   *

I was thinking about .22 caliber bullets. Right through their alligators. The right size for alligators. Some of them would die. They wear them over their hearts. Or is it the other side? Or is the heart in the middle?

Some would die.

Here and there they would fall. Crossing the fairway of the ninth hole, jogging along the dry riverbed, roller-skating by the student union at the university. Two, maybe three, each day. In the busyness of an ordinary day some little blond sophomore from Phoenix or San Diego or nowhere, some fraternity boy walking along with a tennis racket in his hand, will drop to his knees and die of a bullet hole through his shirt.

If I used a silencer, the event would be soundless. Maybe there would be a gasp. "Auk! Aaak! Ghah!"

That would put an end to alligator shirts. An end. Madman on the loose! But what's the point? To puncture a symbol? Or is it a symptom? The same innocent zombies still ambulating around, shirt or no shirt, alligators or no alligators. So much death. *See a shrink*, she said.

That's a laugh.

*   *   *

1

I have what I need to live: a typewriter, a desk, shelves for my books, window shades, a mattress, a fan, a sink, a stove, a toilet. Once I had a stereo. It was stolen. I didn't need it. Still have the records. Bach cello suites, Grieg piano concertos, some Mendelssohn, some Chopin—ugly, useless things. I listen to the fan. Or to silence. Silence suits me more and more. It pulsates. Or am I pulsating? It's all very calming.

The map over the table in the kitchen. I sit at the table and scan the map. Orange India. Yellow China. Green Vietnam, north and south. Something to do. When I eat. When I feel like it. Nothing happens. Saigon is still Saigon on this map. Saigon. Bygone.

No one comes here. No one visits.

* * *

The girl outside the door could be Avon calling. Too much makeup. Why wear any? Makeup. Make-down. Could be a make-down shakedown.

She knows my name. And what big brown eyes she has! Mascara. Liner. Blusher. Rouge. And abundant hair—buff colored—eddying beyond her shoulders. Imagine the time at the mirror.

She extends her hand, cool and bony, like a sea gull. I am supposed to shake the sea gull, I surmise. I give the frail bones a squeeze.

"I'm Jessica Eagan," she says. "William Reese told me about you. *Professor* Reese?"

Professorese.

"I'm sorry to just barge in like this," she says, "but you don't have a phone—at least, I couldn't find a listing for you, and I tried, I really did. And I have to talk with someone and Professor Reese said—"

"*Qu'est-ce que*, Jessica?" I say.

"Huh?"

"You know Reese?" I say.

"I'm taking his class. Humanities 112?"

I'm supposed to respond, but I don't. She keeps talking.

"It isn't even required. Who'd think a course in ethics would turn out to be interesting? I never would've. My big sister—I was in a sorority—she said it was a gut. And, besides, the house's study-room drawers were crammed with humanities papers going back practically to the sixties. . . ."

I let her chat on for a while. It doesn't surprise me that they still let Reese teach a course like that. Ethics. Right up his alley. I can picture him in green pajamas and thin black socks, silk socks, draping his hand over my old lady's breasts while murmuring profundities about moral imperatives or Goodness-in-itself. Raisins.

"Mr. Marcus? Mr. Marcus? Are you all right?"

It's the girl. She has noticed me spacing out. I forget this business of talking to people. I tell her I'm brain damaged. A piece or two of shrapnel in the parietal. She'll have to bring me back to the here-and-now if I drift off. That's all bullshit, of course, but it saves explanations. I have no manners.

"Why did Reese send you here?" I ask.

She flashes a look of impatience. Her eyes tell me she's already explained it all, about Reese, back when I wasn't listening. Here we go again.

"He made us read an essay by a French guy. Phillipe de someone? All about existentialism. It started me thinking. About life, you know? What was my life all about? I tried discussing it with Leslie—my big sister at the house, remember?—about having to choose from one moment to the next even just to *be*, and how we're going to die in the end, but we have to assume responsibility all along. Leslie said I was beginning to sound like some book. She said I was thinking too much. Can you believe that?"

Her eyes check me out for signs of life.

"Your friend thinks you think too much," I say, letting her know I'm still on the line.

"Well, she isn't really my friend anymore. I depledged."

"Come again?"

"I quit the sorority. May I sit down now?"

The door opens into the kitchen. I clear the books and dishes to the other side of the table, and she sits.

"I'm a barbarian," I tell her. "There's coffee, but it's poison."

"You look barbarian," she says.

"The beard?"

"Your eyes."

I never see them.

"I expected you to look like Reese," she says.

"The thin tie? The thin nose? The thin eyes? The thin hair?"

She laughs. I realize that underneath the makeup are signs of intelligent life. Depledged.

"There's rum," I say. "I don't have any milk or sugar."

"That's okay. I'm on a diet."

She watches me look at her body. She's wearing a violet-and-blue-striped jersey—with no alligator—and white cutoffs. Lean, long legs. Her toes, nudging the thongs of her rubber flip-flops, are painted to match her fingernails. Flip-flops.

"You were telling me about Reese," I say, once she has her coffee.

"God, this is bitter."

"It's represso," I tell her.

"It's what?"

"Espresso. The coffee."

"Oh, I can't believe it! You all really do drink it!"

"Who drinks it?"

"You existentialists."

"You think I'm an existentialist?"

"Professor Reese said you're practically the only one left."

How old can she be, this Jessica Eagan? Nineteen?

"I went to Professor Reese's office and told him how taken away I was by that essay by Phillipe de . . . the French one? He said he was pleased that ideas from the course were coming across. I asked him if he was an existentialist."

I have to laugh. Reese an existentialist! He's more of a praying mantis.

"What did he say?"

"He said no one is an existentialist anymore, practically. He called it a cultural phenomenon whose time had gone, like the hippies or art disco. He went on about the French after the Post War being overwhelmed by a German weltonsmog, and the Nazis and the Jews, and how the world has changed. I didn't follow everything. He talked a lot about John Paul Sartre and Alfred Camus . . ."

I leave her reciting the catechism and look over to the map. I fall into Hue, into the Imperial City, just before the first big Tet. The golf course at the Officers' Club. Eighteen holes: regulation size. So green in the light of dawn it might have been in Ireland.

Naturally, being only a grunt, a private, I couldn't play it. But who can tolerate the game of golf? The holes, the little white balls, the scorecards. But to walk the greens just after dawn, mist in the air . . . securing a perimeter. Before the Tet.

After the Tet, everything changed. More sand traps.

The girl is talking on. Something about bad faith. She doesn't need me. I move up the coast. From Hue to Quang Tri, close to the parallel, with black smoke and cordite stinking up the air. And then down from the DMZ along Highway One to Da Nang, craters by the road, craters everywhere after a while, some dry, some filled with mud and God knows what else. Da Nang down to Quang Ngai, carts along the road, flies everywhere, mechanized thunder in the sky, fires in the distance, sheets of fire. And farther down to An Nhon. Down as far as Nha Trang. Nha Trang, where the lieutenant got fragged.

"Is it true?"

She is asking me a question.

"Are you the only existentialist left around here?"

"No one's an existentialist anymore," I tell her. "I'm just depressed sometimes, that's all."

"Depressed?"

"Sure. Did you ever think about that, *Qu'est-ce que*? Maybe existentialism is merely the philosophical symptom of depression."

"My name's not Kessica. It's Jessica. With a *J*."

"Or maybe we should say the philosophical *system* of depression?"

"You're depressed," she says, "because you're born into the world alone, and you know you're going to die, right?"

"I'm depressed," I say, "because I'm surrounded by alligators."

"Alligators?" She looks down the hall off the kitchen into the rest of my little rat hole for confirmation.

"The ones on people's shirts," I tell her. "Totemic ones."

"You're funny," she says. "Professor Reese didn't tell me you were funny."

"He said I'm an existentialist. Isn't that funny?"

"He told me you were interested in philosophy."

"Professor Reese has a long memory."

"Do you ever think about one's dying?" she asks.

"About how awfully slow it comes?" I say. I do think that. It's calming to know that it comes sooner or later. But which is better? Sooner? Or later?

"What about Right Living?" she asks.

"I live off a disability pension."

She tells me again that I'm funny. Her eyes share the joke too, but I don't.

Since she's interested in philosophy, I give her some books. I don't need them. I show her to the door.

"Can I come talk to you again, Mr. Marcus?"

"Why would you want to?" I ask.

"I don't want to. I choose to."

*　　*　　*

He shouldn't have been on a search-and-destroy. Wasn't even infantry-trained. He was in intelligence. Desk job. *Ici on parle francais.* Desk job. He never had to leave Saigon. But he wanted to see action, wanted to move through the countryside. A desk job. Then, when the C.O. bought it, he was next in command. He was a lieutenant. And they weren't even enemy troops. Children. Rotors of the gunship above throwing dust and roaring—no wonder he didn't hear them. Not even the enemy. Just children. And why Willy Peter? Why a white phosphorus grenade? The little bastards in that bunker all aglow like it was Christmas. Auk! Aaak! Ghah! Little slopes with big dark eyes. Two full clips to put them out of their pain. Fucking lieutenant.

*   *   *

She sits across from me at the table and stirs honey into her depresso. It's her honey. No more paint on her fingers and toes. It amazes me that the enamel doesn't cling. She's pretty, it turns out. Her own face. Make-down.

She tells me what she saw yesterday on Jacobus Avenue down near the Thirtieth Street Café. Four girls sat on an adobe wall dangling their legs. They looked like junior-high girls. They all wore knee socks, but they must have traded off because none of the pairs of legs matched up right. Women notice such things. All bright colors. And a boy on the sidewalk was looking at them, a boy holding a skateboard. She couldn't hear them. The boy took one of the girls' hands and shook it. He shook hands with the next girl, and with the next, and with the last. Jessica says he blushed, with her watching him—blushed and walked stiffly off, his elbows punching the air behind him, skateboard and all.

"He wanted to touch one of them," she says. "One only. He couldn't let on, though. So he reached up to them all. Shaking hands was his cover. So he could touch her, the special one. That's why he blushed."

"Maybe he's running for student council," I say.

"They don't have student council that young," she says.

"Maybe he's leaving town."

"I like my version better," she says.

"Have it your way."

"Marcus, it doesn't have to be so grim. He's just a little boy."

"Little boys are grim."

*   *   *

The lieutenant deserved what he got. Six seconds to beat it the hell out of there, and for what anyone knew it could have been the V.C. You don't hear much about the fraggings. It's like all the dope; you hear more about the dope. And the desertions. But not about the fraggings. The grenades. It isn't like he didn't deserve it.

*   *   *

She is referring once again to life. This kind of perception has been a recurring problem lately. It's also the basis of her final paper for Reese's course. She comes here to use my typewriter.

The French existentialists, she argues, have always responded to man's being-in-the-world with despair, noting that each of us is born into the world alone, blah, blah, blah. But why not take delight, she asks, in our being born into the world? We *are* alive, she reminds the reader, she reminds Professorese. She reminds me. She writes: "To live, to merely be here on earth is statistically so improbable given the lonely universe, so astounding, that it's a wonder we don't spend our lives dancing in amazement."

That's what Jessica thinks. I'm happy for her. Or I would be, if I felt that sort of thing. She wishes I would see it her way. What does she know? Soon she'll start hanging plants in my window.

*   *   *

"Marcus," she says, "Reese thinks you wrote that paper."

"Didn't I?"

"Jesus Christ, no! You didn't. All you did was rant and rave about people's illusions while I was trying to type. You remember that? Illusions. How people put alligators over their hearts and go golfing and keep careful scores of all the wrong things."

I don't recall saying those things, but they sound reasonable.

"And all the while," she says, "I kept trying to concentrate— Marcus, are you listening?"

"What makes you think he thinks you cheated?"

"He called me in after class and asked me to define half the words in my paper."

"Did he actually accuse you?"

"He looked at me funny. He stared at me."

"And?"

"And he asked me who Kierkegaard was."

"What did you say?"

"I told him to take a flying leap of faith, and I walked out." I laugh.

"Don't laugh," she says. "He thinks I cheated."

"He doesn't. Don't be so dense. Reese is just testing the bread."

"Testing the bread?"

"He's wondering if you're ready to come out of the oven."

"Huh?"

*   *   *

"How come," *Qu'est-ce que* asks me, "how come if you're a writer you never write anything?"

"Who says I'm a writer?"

"William does."

Now he's William. The course is over. He gave her an *A*.

She tells me they met for lunch at the Thirtieth Street Café.

"What else did he say?" I ask.

"He talked about you."

"What about?"

"That you once were a graduate student, and you used to beat him at chess, in that very bar."

"Is that it?"

"He said he used to live with a woman who was once your friend."

Used to? My *friend*?

"What else?"

"He told me about the war."

"What about it?"

"About the mistake. That you didn't know it was a hospital with kids in it and that the bunker—"

"That wasn't me," I say. "That was the lieutenant."

"He says that you were the lieutenant."

"And that now I should see a shrink?"

"He didn't say that."

A fly buzzes over by the window. Nothing is happening. India is yellow. Burma is purple.

"Marcus, what is it like to kill someone?"

"It's just like killing yourself," I say. "Except you have to live with it."

"Do you want to be dead?"

"You mean physically dead?" I ask.

She walks to the window and draws a line through the grit with her finger. A little shaft of clean sunlight streaks down through the dust in the air.

"Marcus, if I asked you, would you touch me?"

I want to look at her eyes to see what she's getting at, but her back is to me.

"Why?" I ask.

"I want to be real to you."

I have nothing to say. I used to smoke cigarettes, but I don't even have that anymore to fill in the holes.

She turns toward me and undoes her blouse. She says once more that she wants me to touch her. Her hair falls over the blades of her back and over her breasts. It makes me sad because she is young and beautiful, and I have to strain to recall how long it has been since a naked woman has looked into my eyes.

She comes near and puts her hand on my arm. She asks me to touch her.

I understand that she is trying to reach me, but when I touch her breast it feels like rubber in my hand. I take my hand away.

"It doesn't make sense," I tell her.

"Why does is have to mean no, then?" she asks. "Why can't it not make sense and be yes?"

It's no use. She doesn't understand.

*   *   *

She comes by to tell me that she's moving in with Reese. She has come to remove her honey, her plants, her half-shelf of paperback books. It doesn't take her long to clear out.

"Isn't Reese a little old?" I say.

"You mean physically old?" she says, not looking at me. You'd think she was leaving me for him. I recognize the gesture.

I wonder what became of my old lady.

"It won't last forever, you know," I say.

"I don't care."

I tell her she is beginning to sound like me.

"But I'll get over it," she says. "Will you?"

*   *   *

I wonder if Reese thinks of them comparatively. My old lady was emotional, had a flair for histrionics. *Go see a shrink.* She had enough feelings for both of us. At least for a time. Raisins. This other one was just coming into bloom, just blossoming. And still alive. Still alive now.

People have a troubling effect on me, though. Maybe I should live away from people. Someplace with no doors. Just a vent. Or a window. A window with bars.

It's consoling to think that I did her no harm. Or it would be consoling if I felt such things.

A Bad Winter
Just East
of Show Low

His wife was a writer, a poet, and the dog was supposed
to make her feel safe. But now she was in the state hospital,
and he was left with the dog. It was daybreak, and he was out
with the dog. The earth was freezing over for winter, and the
dead dry leaves lay on the ground. This was up in the mountains, just east of Pinetop and Show Low, where it gets cold.
He stretched his gaze over the line of slag piles as he walked,
while the dog, nosing through the rocks and boulders for gar-
bage, went ahead. The dog circled toward the footbridge, and
on a grassy rise he hunkered down to chew on something—
some white paper. Catching sight, the man started for the dog,
shaking his fists and yelling. He ran for the dog, disgusted at
having to pay time and time again to have him wormed. The
dog looked like an Airedale, but smaller, almost a miniature.
When the man drew close, the dog leapt away, leaving the
scrap of paper behind. But it wasn't paper, the man saw. It
was a little white animal. A dead animal. A dead rat. The man
felt sick.

His name was Smith, and he was due at work at ten. He
worked in an elementary school library, and his job depressed
him. He collated cards into the card catalog. The school was in
a mining town, and there was no money for organizing the
library holdings by computer. No money and no interest. A
single unit with a simple video display screen could make his
job obsolete. When the job was finished, he would be obsolete
anyway. He was thirty-five years old, and he didn't have to
wear a tie. And there would be other jobs. He had taken this
job thinking what he had always thought taking jobs, that it
would put bread and beans on the table and let them live

somewhere quiet while he and his wife concentrated on the important things.

He was no longer sure that anything about his life was important, but for his wife it meant her writing. She often wrote before dawn. She had insomnia so it was all the same to her. Dawn. Midnight. She was often bucked out of what little sleep she did get by nightmares. She called them night-stallions. Nightbroncos. He never had nightmares. She didn't share hers. She said she couldn't remember them. He thought that she was lying. He thought that she was afraid to tell him. She was exhausted most of the time.

In the last few weeks, she had become terrified of leaving their place, the broken-down, two-room house they rented so cheaply, the house with its long view down the canyon. And before that she had panicked just pushing a cart through the aisles of the Safeway, or sitting in the theater in Show Low, just sitting in the dark. His wife was a small woman with small hands. Her parents were Japanese, but she was from Oregon. Her poems were as clean and grim as white bones and broken teeth. In the last months nearly a dozen had been taken for publication.

Smith stood in increasing awe of her talent. It shamed him secretly that he slept so well and so regularly. He never had nightmares. He never had dreams. Or if he did, he didn't recall them. He woke every day before seven and didn't need an alarm clock. Back at the university, where they had met, he had taken English and written some poetry. He had had some clever ideas about poetry, too. But he had discussed his ideas too many times since then, and they were no longer clever. He still read books in the evening and subscribed to reviews that came in the mail from New York. Now and then, he tried his luck at the typewriter but could squeeze nothing out of his life but banalities. He would rip the sheet from the carriage and crumple and toss it in frustration. The dog would go for it, smiling.

Now he stood in the cold morning, steaming the air, staring

down, not at the white paper, but at a rat on the frozen ground. The dog waited at a distance to see if his anger would pass. Smith could tell that the dog wanted another go at the dead animal. What he should do is pick the rat up and drop it off the bridge into the dark creek. Maybe lift it by its long tail. A skin of ice had already formed over much of the stream, but under the bridge the current was too strong. By summer the creek bed would be dry. Summer was a long way off. Smith nudged the dead animal with his boot. It was heavy and stiff. Dead weight.

He didn't want to touch the animal, even with gloves on. He didn't want it near his eyes. He didn't like dead things. Dead things made him hunch his back. He imagined invisible mites infesting his gloves, invading his touch, his fingers. He hunched his back and shuddered. He stared at the aspens by the creek and hugged his own chest. Others would pass this way, he thought, people native to the land. Let one of them toss the rat.

He shooed the reluctant dog over the bridge and walked beyond, among the slag heaps and piles of deposited rock from the copper operations. Waste rock. He hadn't come close to touching the rat, but his hands felt soiled. He raised his hands and eyed the palms of his gloves.

He remembered that Tadaye, his wife, had lifted a bird to her eyes that way once. It was in Oregon in the open fields of her parents' seed nursery. They had been caught in a downpour, he and Tad, and there was a shed. A bird had trapped itself inside and was trying to escape into the light. The bird hurled itself again and again against the one, dust-coated window. He and his wife had startled the bird into ever more desperate attempts until it fell to the dirt stunned. The rain pounded on the roof, and the air was old.

She had cupped the speckled thing in her hand, and then it fanned in the gentle cage of her fingers. It became a flower for her, a wild thing. He hadn't wanted to touch it. It could have lice. He remembered that. He could still picture its skin, its bald spots where feathers had been lost. Don't birds carry lice? Isn't that why vultures have bald heads? To avoid picking up even more lice when they dip into carrion?

But the bird had fluttered into a flower for her, and he had envied her. He could even sense the weightlessness of the creature in her hands, its tingling. Outside she had swept it back into the brightening sky as though it had been a part of herself.

The dog wanted him to throw a stick. He had no qualms about sticks, although once the dog got started there was no end to it. He threw the stick into the woods, and the dog crashed through the undergrowth. Lots of poets have breakdowns, he reminded himself. Lots of poets have crazy periods. Look at Lowell. Look at Plath. Look at all the ones who killed themselves.

He didn't pursue that line of thought.

*   *   *

Smith sat at his little desk in the library, a child's desk, the JAI to JUL card drawer on his left, a pile of new, white cards at his fingers. He was perched in one of the four window-alcoves, with a view of the reading circle, the check-out desk, the study tables, and the books for new readers. The wood finishings and old books smelled of permanence and serenity, and the steam was up. Smith could hear it hissing. Mrs. Molino, his boss, was reading to the third graders. The children were giggling and teasing each other, as though they thought they'd be young forever. Smith remembered the days when he thought of winter as a magical time, with sleds and snow hills and no two snowflakes alike. He had believed that, that no two snowflakes were exactly alike. Now he was sure that plenty were alike. In fact, most were alike. Exactly alike. It was utter nonsense. He remembered thinking that winter stayed outside when you came indoors. Now he felt like crying.

Mrs. Molino walked over to let him know that she was worried for his sake. It was a true pity. Still, he had to be strong for Tadaye, right? He still had to eat, right? Mrs. Molino was built squat and sturdy like a giant mother quail.

"I see you!" she shouted, catching one of the third-grade boys in the act. "That is not how we behave in our library!"

The little boy sat down and pretended to be ashamed. Everyone liked Mrs. Molino, but she had her limits. You didn't want to get on her bad side. Life was that simple.

She turned back to Smith. "Do they say what is the matter with her?" She used the same voice when she was fixing a Band-Aid to a child's knee. It didn't make any difference how old or young Smith was. God knows, the whole world could use some mothering, no? Smith wished he could help, but the wound was too big for one Band-Aid. Mrs. Molino was like a hearth, but he was out in the snow.

Smith didn't know what was wrong with his wife. Every time, the diagnosis was different. Different and longer. But the pills were the same: tranquilizers, antidepressants, antipsychotics, Amitril, Librium, Compazine, Triavil. One or the other. When she took these, she didn't write poetry. She became just like him. It was only a matter of time before she went off her medications though. He was stuck with it.

On the wall of the library, Pancho Villa rode through the dust of one poster. A toothbrush gave the three steps to dental hygiene on another. And one showed the red light and the green light. Smith turned back to the JAI to JUL catalog cards, fingering through the drawer to find his place. He had never needed medications to put a stop to a line of thought.

*   *   *

The dead rat was out there still, on the grass beside the bridge, and Smith stood above it, shooing off the dogs. His dog whined and couldn't keep his stub of tail still. The dog looked from the dead rat to Smith's eyes and back to the dead rat. He wanted to get his jaws on the thing. The other two dogs, both black monsters with high, muscular shoulders and tails that stretched toward the sky, were just as eager.

Smith wished someone would show up to take them in hand. Probably they were strays though. If he moved from that spot, the dogs would tear the rat apart. He might control his dog, but not the other two. He didn't know why that should matter to him, what stray dogs got into, but it did.

The bridge, with its splintery wood planking and black iron guardrail, was only twenty or twenty-five steps away. He looked at his gloves, the leather palms clean and new, and then down at the rat, which held up its fragile pink paws in a useless, indecipherable gesture. Its eyes were gems staring off into the evening sky. Smith bent close, looking for teeth marks. He was surprised it hadn't been ripped into pieces by one set of jaws or another. There was no smell, nothing but the odor of the dirt dusted with snow. He nudged it with his boot, and it was now rock hard. What a strong lock death holds us in, he thought. The dogs were whining, and night was coming on. Smith had a bus to catch. He looked toward the bridge and the black pool of open water beneath it. He thought that even from here he could hurl the rat into the water, but at the briefest touch he recoiled. He shuddered. He couldn't do it. He charged into the dogs, and they scattered. He got his own dog across the bridge with him and didn't look back.

*   *   *

The hospital was down in the city, over an hour and a half away by bus. Between the bus schedule and the limited visiting hours, Smith could see her for maybe half an hour. Then he might have to wait half the night for the return bus. There was a place on Thirtieth Street that was open all night, a quiet place where he could sit over a beer and wait. Going down, waiting, coming back. It kept him busy. If he just kept busy, he didn't feel the holes in his life. Diesel exhaust queered the air, and Smith was glad he wasn't driving. The others on the bus looked poor and humble and exhausted from the mines. Smith realized that he looked poor and humble too. He was becoming poor and humble. And his wife was in the state hospital. It was the times. It was the economy. He wasn't immune. Why should he be immune? No one was reading the newspaper on the bus. The news didn't matter, did it? No one was talking. It was quiet.

He walked down the long, lonely path to the building housing Ward Five, a large, adobe block of Spanish design. By day, the walls of the building showed up pink in the hot sun, but now, at night, they were gray. He thought he saw jack rabbits moving in the shadows and behind the bushes along the path. It was chilly even here in this city built up out of the desert floor.

The corridor with its yellow lights was like a tunnel. The walls were of glazed, yellow brick. Old insulated pipes ran under the ceiling, some of them tapping peculiarly and dripping here and there onto the floor. At the attendant's station, he gave his wife's name. The duty nurse, who looked enough like Mrs. Molino to be her sister, told him to wait.

She came down the yellow corridor, his wife, wearing her own clothes, her blue jeans bagging, her black coat tight, tugging at the buttons. Her hair looked funny, as though someone else had brushed it, and her smile was distant and somehow not attached to anything. Smith didn't know if he should hug her right there in front of the attendant's station or save it. He wanted to hold her, but didn't.

She was given permission to go off the ward, and Smith held her tight under a big cottonwood tree on the grounds. The moon was rising. They sat atop a picnic table. She told him she had been outside that day. Before. In group. Sometimes they did things like that. They had tried to have a game and threw a ball around. Some of them did. Not her. The men had gone on and on about shooting animals. You know how men are. One man chipped a rock at a rabbit. They started telling about shooting rabbits. Rabbits, coyotes, road runners. So I said, why don't you toss some dynamite at them? Why don't you blast them with dynamite?

The doctors? They were okay, but they didn't know. Yes, she was sleeping, but it gave her cotton-mouth, and she was so dry inside. Her intestines were ropes made of straw. And they kept taking blood from her arms. Would it ever stop? It was driving her crazy. She was tired of circling in circles. Tired of knocking against walls.

Smith had brought her a chocolate bar. She didn't eat candy when she wasn't in the hospital, but sometimes she got a hunger for chocolate. He remembered that from the other times. It had to do with the medications, he thought.

She took the candy bar and peeled it like a banana. "Are you going to want me back?" She sounded like a child. "Will you want me back?"

Of course he would. He would always. She was safe with him. He cupped her face in his hands, his little bird. "Don't touch me that way," she said. He dropped his hands. That's the medication talking, he told himself. That's just the medication.

Then she was cold. It was too cold to sit outside. She had been frightened that he wouldn't come, and now she was relieved. She had been frightened of being left alone, but now she was cold.

*　　*　　*

Smith shivered in the cold. The moon was high. It was very late, and the dog seemed even smaller than before. Away in the distance the dead rat waited, white as moonlight.

It wouldn't be difficult. He was prepared. He made his way to the grassy mound, and he could hear the black waters curdling under the bridge. The dog whimpered but stayed at his side. Smith had his gloves on and was clumsy fishing a plastic bag from his pocket. He had started saving bags from the produce section of the Safeway. The white rat waited in death, unbroken by dogs or daylight. The moon caught in its eye. The man kicked it into the plastic bag.

He picked up the bag by its corner and held it high in the air. The rat's eye bulged in the bottom. He carried it to the footbridge and dropped it over the side. The water was black. Smith saw the rat slipping away. It wouldn't be long before the waters froze over entirely. The children could come and skate the ice through a veil of infinite snowflakes and never know. The rat wouldn't be there. The rat would be gone. A better man might have taken off his gloves for the rat, he knew. A poet would have shaken hands with that worst death, a cold death, but Smith was no poet. But he had been picked out for the dead rat, and, in his own way, he had taken care of everything. It was late, and it had taken all day, but he had taken care of everything.

An Infidelity

24 January. This was while I was watching television. She was one of those vaguely foreign, ageless blondes, an actress of some sort, part of a pair of sisters. What she said was ridiculous, just celebrity quiz-show chatter. But now I can't shake it out of my head. If you stuff a jar with dollar bills, one for whenever you make love during the first year of marriage, she said, and if you remove a dollar every time after the first year, you'll never go flat broke. Why should this be on my mind all day? Betty and I aren't even married.

But we don't put much of a drain on the jar. And look how tediously steady we've become! It's been over two years now. Over *three* years. Steady and stable. For months she's been working nights over at that Thirtieth Street Café, and now we've got frozen steaks stored up in the ice box, we've had the engine on the Chevy overhauled, we buy brandy by the case, and we still get the rent check in the mail by the first, month after month.

(And all this despite my getting only three calls since the New Year. What is it, anyway? Regular teachers don't get sick this time of year in Arizona? Did the baby boom finally peter out last week?)

With things running so slowly, I've been letting my beard come in. And instead of working, I've been tinkering at my journal here. That's the word for it—tinkering, trying to make sense of my life. Should I try to find a more dependable line of work? Should I try to finish the damned dissertation after all? What?

I ran four miles today.

25 January. Betty's been short with me lately. I'm not surprised. She gets impatient, coming home at one, one-thirty, bitching because her feet hurt (or her back or her head) and the tips have been meager. Or because Larry wanted her to push the salad plate because the lettuce was starting to rust—and half the customers grew recalcitrant, then sullen and stingy.

She's been complaining about it for a long time now, how she works so hard, and how there's never time really to talk to or know anyone. She has needs too, she says. And then, when she gets home and she's too tired even to think, she finds me here, innocent as the dust, scribbling on the kitchen table, waving her off with my other hand, saying, "Wait a minute, Betty, I'll be right with you," while I finish calculating how of the last 365 days I've gone jogging on 269, which works out to 74 percent of the year. "Listen to this," I say, but Betty cups her hands over her ears and says, "How come it never occurs to you to set out some brandy for me when I get home?"

And what about washing the dishes heaped in the sink or doing some shopping or getting the laundry done? She's perfectly right, of course. I should be more thoughtful, but I keep getting caught up in things, in these journals.

Consider five years ago today. I was teaching at a little community college back East, filling in for someone taking a sabbatical. It wasn't much of a job. Paid nothing. I don't remember the details, but I have a weak memory. I was teaching business math. Or maybe basic accounting. I do remember one student, a girl who presented herself at my apartment door one night. This was before I knew Betty. Was I really surprised to see her, this kid? In class she always sat by the door in back, probably because she came late. The classrooms were barely furnished, with just the green chalkboard and retractable movie screen up front. No podium, no desk, no American flag. A low-budget school. She never said much in class. Tapped her long, painted fingernails on the tiny deskette. Not impatient taps but bored taps, unconscious taps. And chewed gum. No, not gum. She used to smoke cigarettes (in violation of the rules, no doubt) and watch me in a manner I can only describe as slinky. What was her name? I'm sure it's written down somewhere. I've kept my grade books.

The way she smoked, sensual and unhurried, you'd think no smoke was involved, only pastel clouds. She drew on a cigarette as though she thought talent scouts might be in the room. Had she been taller, she might have passed as a fashion model. She had the bones for it. She was thin and shadowy, not the buxom type like Betty. She was freckled as well, but on her the tawny spots brought to mind neither cornflowers nor childhood but, rather, leopards.

If I had a policy about socializing with students, I can't recall it now. I must have avoided them. Can't always tell when one is sharking for a grade. But this one, leaning against the door of my apartment with suave confidence, was pulling an A-minus on her own. And she was interesting.

She aspired to be an actress. In fact, she conversed entirely by delivering lines. She made the question "May I come in?" entirely rhetorical.

What was her name? Bertina? Barona? Something like that. Bezille?

She had some fairly traditional lines: "You live here by yourself?"

"Christ, you have a lot of books."

"Mind if I smoke?"

"Black, no sugar."

After I brought the coffee, she vacated the armchair to join me on the deep, plunging sofa—ostensibly to share the coffee table.

Even instructors as unfatherly as I was are occasionally made targets for thinly disguised cries for help, and on the off chance that she had some such "hidden agenda," I left her space to bring it forward.

"Well, Bezille," I said, "I'm a little surprised to see you here."

"Only a little?" she said, touching her fingertip to her perfect chin.

So much for that theory. She was soon at it again with her silken cigarettes, which, I was able to note, were mentholated. Back then I was still a smoker, but I smoked straight

Camels. Mainly Camels. Marlboros, Raleighs, Pall Malls too. You name it. Smoking was always such a delight. But not mentholated cigarettes.

Bezille had a question for me, though, which made me think I'd discarded the cry-for-help hypothesis prematurely.

"What do you think of someone who is having an affair behind her boyfriend's back?"

"What do you think about it?" I parried, not having suffered four years of adolescent psychotherapy for nothing.

She was probably staring at her fingernails when we got to this point, at her maroon nailpolish. She looked up at me, showed me her slender tongue, and said, "I think it's fun."

Now here was a woman who wasn't letting life pass her by. She probably aspired to be not merely an actress but a *French* actress. She wanted *un amour furieux*. Fire, passion, pyrotechnics. And she wanted to know what I was going to do about it. She slipped out of her sandals and curled her feet under her thighs on the sofa. She raised her hand and put her fingers ever so gently on . . .

Ah! That will be Betty on the stairs. Better close here and see about that glass of brandy. Ran 3.4 miles.

26 January. Betty came home in a good mood last night. Great tips (typical Friday). Wanted to go out for a late one "like we used to." I explained that I was feeling preoccupied. "Been at it again?" she wanted to know. I reminded her that if I didn't write things down I'd lose them. My life would slip through my fingers. She calls this my "bathroom drain theory." She laughs, but with my memory that's a good analogy.

Of course, she doesn't buy any of it. "Come off it, Freddy," she says. "There's nothing wrong with your memory. Your problem is you don't pay attention to the here-and-now."

What does she know about it?

I ran four and a half miles today, putting me fifteen miles ahead of where I was at this point last January. Today is the one thousand, one hundred twenty-first day since I last put a cigarette to my lips. Three years, twenty-six days. No one could argue that I lack willpower.

27 January. Last night in a dream, I got married. It was an anxiety dream. The bride was someone I didn't know. I had never seen her before. She was Mexican or something. Possible Romanian. We couldn't speak the same language. It was a hot night and well-wishers were crowding around us in a plain white room. A woman in a scarf, supposedly my friend, kept trying to convince me that it was okay. I should marry her, she said; I'd be happy.

She turned out to be the girl's sister. "Marry her. You'll see!" she said. I gave in. I married her. The girl's eyes wouldn't meet mine.

Then we were alone in the white room. It was suffocatingly hot. She wore just a slip, and from under her arms stiff black hairs stood out. In the dream, I realized that her little hairs were blameless. She had a dull look, as though she had been stunned or drugged.

In bed it was too hot even for sheets. We lay there staring at the ceiling, not touching. I smoked a Camel. I didn't know her name. I was lonely.

In the dream, I thought I had had this dream before. But now, awake, I'm not sure. I must remember to keep track of my dreams so I can tell for sure.

That Camel was the only good part.

A call came today from Mansfield Junior High, but I turned them down. I wanted to think.

28 January. I cleaned the bathroom today, sure to please Betty. I noticed it's beginning to look like a beard. In the mirror it looks green to me, but Betty says that's my imagination. Years ago, back in college, I kept track of the number of women I made love with. The thing of it was, the rate always picked up when I had a beard. To this day, I have no idea whether my average was low or high. (By my count, it was four and two-thirds different women each year after my freshman year.)

I recall one time, my junior year, I think, that I went to the new Pewter Pot in Central Square with Dave and Nina. I was at B.U., but Dave, who went to Antioch, was in Cambridge living off a work-study job. Anyway, there we were in the Pewter Pot, its wallpaper depicting the Boston Tea Party, the air heavy with the warm smells of muffins baking, and the two of them, David and Nina, were going at it pretty vituperatively about a play we'd just seen at the Loeb Theater. "You can't do that," David was saying. "If Beckett knew they were casting Lucky as an Indian, he'd turn over in his grave."

"It's a 'Native American,' not an 'Indian,'" said Nina, poking him in the shoulder, "and I don't see why they can't make a social statement."

"Why not let a paraplegic have the part then?" said David, rolling out his palms. "Why not let the Easter Seal Child do it?" He turned to our waitress, approaching our table with double orders of cranberry nut muffins and coffee, and said, "Christ, Beckett would turn over in his grave."

"What are you talking about?" she said, dumping down her tray. "Beckett's not dead." It turned out she had just finished a degree in drama at the University of Michigan, and this job was the closest thing to acting she could find. Her name was Daisy.

Actually, her name was Renee, but her Pewter Pot name tag read Daisy, and that's what I called her. (It turned out that none of the waitresses at the Pewter Pot was named what you thought.) Not long afterward, Daisy and I became lovers. I should dig up the journal from that year. I don't remember how we got from *A* to *B*, but I remember *B*-ing in my college room with her one sunny afternoon. She was serious about love. Well, not so much serious as quiet. She drew the shade, and the light became pearly. Music from someone's stereo filtered down the hall, soft and muted and bluesy. She took off her blouse and was wonderfully thin. She had delicate veins that looked like streaks of cobalt under her skin, and her ribs and breasts were so delicate that you had to be gentle to hold them. Naked, she might have stepped from a still life. She didn't laugh or smile. She reached up to my beard. She put her fingers to my cheek.

Did I have a beard when I met Betty? I think I did. She wondered how I'd look without it. So, it's been more than three years.

I promised I'd go for some things before she gets home: orange juice, Pepto Dismal, Maxi-Pads. I think I'll wrap it up here and drive to the 7-11. I ran four miles today.

29 January. Yesterday was Betty's birthday and I forgot. She told me that since I hadn't mentioned it all day, she figured I'd have some surprise for her when she got home. Orange juice, Pepto Bismol, and Maxi-Pads weren't all that she could have hoped for apparently.

It could have been worse. Someone at work, I guess, gave Betty a rose. A delicate, long-stemmed, red rose. It's just the kind of thing she likes. At least someone remembered.

I explained that I don't intentionally forget these things. She wanted to know why I couldn't just look it up in my "precious journal." I tried to tell her that I was back in my college phase yesterday, back before I knew her. She wasn't interested. I blew it.

I ran five miles today at the track around the high school up the street. There's still light in the sky past six o'clock. I called Pueblo High School to remind them I'm available.

30 January. I promised Betty I'd go to the laundromat tonight. I've got enough socks and underwear to last three weeks, but when Betty has her period she runs through her panties in no time. I tell her to get extra pairs, but she says it's more economical to wash them in the bathroom sink at night. But she's always too knocked out, and I end up going to the laundromat.

It's a tiresome, neutral place. Nothing special. A row of washers, top loaders, all a glossy maroon color, and a row of white dryers. PO-NIOC is stenciled over the glass door. A temperamental bill-changer, obsessively insistent upon crisp, uncurled dollar bills. Plastic chairs welded in a form-fitting, patio-green row. No music. No customers usually. Second-rate graffiti on the walls: "Rafael Lobos was here," things like that.

Last time there, I saw that someone had taped up an ad offering music for weddings. "Accordion music for all types of ceremonies." Thinking about it, about the hired accordionist at the wedding, nauseated me. I could imagine the entire asphyxiating thing. Polish weddings. Greek weddings. Cubans. Chicanos in flowery dresses that they buy down in Nogales. Jewish weddings. An equal opportunity. If Betty and I ever get married . . . Can I picture it? The little man with his big chromed accordion. "So, my children, my friends! You should let me know what is your favorite song. Tell me, I'll play it." Betty's mother relieved at last. Circle dances. Betty and I doing the *hora. Hava Nagila!*

Enough.

30 January, late. Betty's usually home by now. What's keeping her? Wednesday nights are usually slow.

But you never know. The laundromat tonight was almost crowded, and I've never seen that before.

An interesting woman was there. I was trying to get the bill-changer to swallow a single (I had four with me), and the machine rejected one after the other. This woman said, "You can get change over there at the Whataburger." I hadn't said anything to her; I hadn't even looked at her. I've trained myself not to look women over. Betty doesn't like it when men stare at her. This woman looked at me very directly, very plainly. It embarrassed me, but it was just a plain look. If she conveyed anything with it, with that look, it was simple human acceptance: Here we are, you and I, adult earthlings at the laundromat. Her hair was drawn efficiently back, away from her face. No make up. An artist might have chosen her as a model, a model for humanity perhaps.

At the Whataburger, I felt uncomfortable troubling the counter girl for two dollars in change, so I ordered coffee to go as well. I thought of bringing back a cup for the woman in the laundromat, but I couldn't picture it. "Hi. Thanks for the tip about getting change. I brought you this. Do you come here often?" Or, "I hope you don't mind. I figured you for black, no sugar." Funny. It's been more than three years since I've worried whether something sounded like a line.

Back at the laundromat, I sorted our stuff into whites and colors, loading up one machine with each pile. I couldn't remember which gets washed in hot water, whites or colors. I read through the instructions on the machine but discovered only that I should have added the detergent before loading. Live and learn. I thought of asking the woman about it, but the same awkwardness stopped me. I'm simply too well-trained to disturb the calm surface of anonymity. I punched my coins into the two machines and dialed both selectors to warm.

Across the room, some other women were folding clothes. Someone's little boy, his elbow covered with grimy Band-Aids, rolled a toy truck along the floor and made engine noises, shifting into low gear and then back-firing. A fellow in an army jacket sat on a rumbling washer reading the *Arizona Daily Star*. I walked over to the row of plastic seats where the woman and some other people sat. The woman smiled. She held my eyes. I felt a moment of panic and didn't recover in time to smile back at her. I took the only seat available, the one next to hers. I could have talked to her but didn't. I sipped my coffee.

She was reading a magazine. I couldn't tell which. I thought it might be *People* and wondered if she were reading about Yoko Ono or John Belushi. She was wearing a denim skirt and had nice legs. She was lean, and the muscles of her legs were articulated. She works on her feet all day, I guessed, probably at the Whataburger. She's married to a man who drives a semi, and he thinks about sending away C.O.D. for the eight-track tapes advertised on television. *Roy Orbison's Greatest Hits*. The little boy roaring across the floor with his truck is probably hers, and she neglects him. She's bored with her life. Hence, her smile. Hence, the way she looked at me.

I started imagining having an affair with her. We would

bring our laundry bags back to my place; Betty wouldn't be home for a couple of hours. The bags of hot clothes could cool off together in a corner.

But I don't have anything by Roy Orbison. There would be no Cold Duck in the refrigerator. And there was the problem of her kid. Where would he go? And what would we talk about? I don't read *People* magazine. Her kid would probably leave his truck behind for Betty to find or else he would tell his old man about it, and there I'd be . . .

But maybe hers were dancer's legs. Maybe she studies interpretive dance or ballet? I looked at her as she read and couldn't imagine her using her fine jawline even to chew gum. She had a simplicity and purity about her that ruled out everything: curlers, daytime television, truck-driving men. Maybe it was *Harper's* she was reading or *Art West*. Maybe she wasn't reading at all, only daydreaming?

She turned to her bag and found a cigarette. Soon smoke curled in front of her and made swirls that stood out against her black sweater. The fragrance of the burning tobacco, sirenlike, called out to me like an old friend.

The way she held her cigarette reminded me of a former student, someone I was thinking about just the other day. Barona? Bezille? I couldn't help watching her as she drew on her cigarette, sensual and unhurried.

I could picture her sitting up in bed in a quiet room, her hands gently on her knees, her presence saying simply, I'm here, I'm here, I'm here. I could imagine touching her face and looking into those guileless eyes. What would I find there if not myself? A way forward? A genuine next step?

She put the magazine aside—it was *High Times*—and was smoking and staring off at the row of dryers. Her hands were small and fine. No rings.

She sensed me watching her, and I looked away. The little boy was whining into the knees of a woman folding clothes. The young guy with the newspaper dropped a purple sock on his way to the dryer, but no one called out to tell him. The sock lay on the floor.

The woman asked me if the smoke bothered me.

"I like it," I said.

"Want one?" she asked, looking into my eyes.

I told her no. I said I wanted to, but it had been over three years now.

That was it. I got up to put my clothes in a dryer, and then I had to unload someone else's things to make space for my own. By the time I returned to my seat, she was gone.

She left something behind. I noticed it on her seat. It was a cigarette. A Lucky. I pocketed it.

31 January. Betty didn't come home at all last night. I find what's happening hard to believe. She phoned today and told me to clear my stuff out. She doesn't know why she's put up with me for so long. She says I should have seen it coming, that if I'd pay a little attention to the here-and-now I'd have seen what was going on.

I don't know where I'll go. I have to think.

For what it's worth, I ran a total of seventy-two miles this month. Eighteen miles more than last January. I weigh one hundred sixty-four pounds.

It's been one day since I smoked my last cigarette.

Mailman

The man in 319 came out to get the mail. Always before it had been the woman or no one. I had never seen the man, but, of course, I had handled his mail. He came down the walk and reached over the cast-iron gate, taking the envelopes without looking at them. Most people look at them. *He* looked at me. His eyes were tired, the lids thick and heavy. "My wife is unfaithful," he said and walked back into 319.

I was surprised to learn that the woman in 319 had been unfaithful. It made me happy. Like all the others living between Central and Lomos, she received the big, glossy sale notices from Taco Bell and the Zodys chain. Like the others, she played the magazine distributors' promotional sweepstakes. Was this her life? Was this all? I was happy to hear that it wasn't.

She was not a beautiful woman. When she was young, she might have been pretty, but her face had no color, her body had no shape. Now, she was a fish. Her eyes were pale-blue disks, large and shallow, and her lips were puffy and round. Perhaps she was myopic. She drifted out for the mail with the composure of a slow-moving bass on a hot day. As she took her mail, she would comment on the weather. "What a hot day." "Not much of a day." "What a dry day." Then she would swim back.

So, when the man in 319 said that his wife had been unfaithful, I was not sorry, except for him. It's hard on the man. Everyone knows that. But I was still happy. It made life less routine. Less routine and bigger. It was better than I had thought, better for us all.

Their name was Smith. They were the Smiths, Nora and Earl. My name is Cruz, which out here is even more common a name than Smith. Of course, few people along the route know my name. But what of that?

It was Smith who came out for the mail from then on. He wasn't looking out for himself, I could see that. For three days he wore the same dirty shirt, a torn t-shirt with "30th Street Regulars" stenciled on it in red letters. It looked like an old, softball-team shirt, a Sunday league shirt. Smith wasn't shaving much either.

He fingered his letters with care now, as though looking for something in particular. One day, I handed over a phone bill, a circular from the Heart Association, and a copy of *Arizona Highways* with a giant saguaro cactus blooming on the cover. The next day it was a business letter postmarked Tucson and a single postcard showing a cable car on Powell Street. The card was from Bill and Doris who were "having a great time despite the rain and thinking of you."

The following day, I brought a seed catalog, a Congressional report (machine franked), a bank statement, and a pale-blue envelope for Nora Smith—an envelope addressed in a bold, masculine hand, the letters large and thick. It bore the local postmark.

I kept the blue letter in my bag. I had a feeling about it. It could always become lost in the mail. It could get misrouted to the regional station down in El Paso.

I handed Smith the rest of it. He looked over the pile and turned his eyes to me. His eyes were sad, pleading for brotherhood.

"I have a pistol," he said. "A thirty-eight. The cylinder spins."

"Why don't you get some sleep?" I told him. "You look like you need some sleep."

"I have hollow-point bullets. Do you know what hollow-point bullets can do to a man's head?"

I told him again to get some sleep. He retreated into his house, saying, "It's nickel plated."

It takes a man time to get over this kind of thing. I've seen it before. It must be rough for her in there, poor fish, but it was better. I stood for a while at the gate. I scanned the windows for a glimpse of her, thinking I would see a fin glide across the glass. Nothing.

An old lawnmower was leaning against the side of the house. The grass was parched blond in a few spots. In this climate, grass goes fast if you don't watch it.

The next day was Saturday, and nothing lay in my bag for 319 except the pale-blue envelope. I passed the place before eleven o'clock, seeing neither of them. The lawn sprinklers were on at 317 and at 321. In fact, sprinklers were running up and down the street, but the lawn at 319 was turning brown.

On Monday, he was there again, his shoulders hunched, his gait slow. He didn't glance at the envelopes. He looked beyond me. "You should have seen her last night," he said. "They were all having her. One after another. Everyone. All of them. And what do you think she did when it was over? She leaned against the worst one, the leader, and kissed him. She said, 'You're better than any man I've ever been to bed with.' The bitch. You should have seen it."

"Where is she now?" I asked.

"With them. With him."

The next day, no one came for the mail. I left it in their box and walked on. I expected to read about the Smiths in the paper. I could imagine the headlines. But nothing was in the paper.

The following day, *she* came out for the mail, looking the same as ever, her faded housedress moving slightly in the hot air, her flat slippers slapping against the cement path.

"What a hot day," she said.

"I haven't seen you in a long time, Mrs. Smith."

She looked at me with her vague blue eyes and breathed out oxygen bubbles. "I've been away," she said. "To Ohio. My people are back in Cleveland."

It was true. They often got mail from Cleveland.

"Where is Mr. Smith?" I asked.

"At work. Where else?"

I gave her the mail and with it the blue envelope. She looked at the writing and said, "It's from my husband. What would he be writing to me for?"

She opened it right there. I should have moved on to 317. "It's a love note. He hasn't even signed it. I bet he missed me."

People are an interesting breed. They will surprise you. It makes life bigger, I have to say, it makes life bigger.

The next day two police cruisers were parked helter-skelter outside 319, blue lights flashing. Women and children from up and down the street stood along the fence. The woman from 317, her hair in curlers, was explaining that he had been yelling all night about "her goddamned love letters lying around the house." She had heard something that could have been a shot. She wasn't sure; she had never heard a shot before. But what could she do? She should have called the police even sooner.

Sirens wailed in the distance. Another police car arrived carrying, in addition to the driver, a man in a dark suit, a tall man who made his way purposefully into the house. An ambulance came, the crew rushing into 319 with a stretcher. The whiteness of the medics' clothing was intense in the sunlight. The metallic voices of the police radios snarled into the air. The neighborhood women stopped talking and just waited.

Then the stretcher was wheeled back out. The body on it was covered, and the crew was in no rush. The sheet was stained on one end. The ambulance drove off without blaring its siren. The woman from 317 held her hand to her mouth.

The man in the dark suit came out into the light with his arm supporting Mrs. Smith. The uniformed officers cleared the gate, asking everyone to please go home now. People backed off a few steps. Mrs. Smith drifted through the confusion like a stunned tuna.

I was sorry for what Smith had done. Everyone was. A short notice appeared in the paper. I was also sorry about Mrs. Smith. It would have been better if she had had a lover. I was sorry about that. That would have been better. She went back to Cleveland. Her mail is forwarded to Cleveland now, at least the first-class mail. The Taco Bell promotionals, the magazine sweepstakes, the shopping mall circulars, and all the rest of the junk gets dumped. We don't forward the junk mail. But she won't miss it. Her people in Ohio must get their own. Why would it be any different in Cleveland?

Benny and I

When the bus came, the driver said he wasn't going to let us on with that shotgun.

"Why not?" asked Benny. "We're old enough."

"Look, son . . ." the driver began.

Benny cut him off. "I'm not your son!"

"Okay, young fellow, take it easy. Now, you see all these folks on the bus? You bring a shotgun on and you'll scare them out of their wits."

We looked into the bus. I could see eight or ten people dressed like they were coming back from church. They stared at me and Benny, which wasn't surprising considering the big deal the driver was making.

We had been waiting at the bus stop for more than an hour, trying to keep warm. It was Sunday morning after we had finished Benny's route. Benny had struck matches to his pocket warmer, but the wind was too strong. When he finally got it going, it was too hot to hold for more than a couple of seconds, even with gloves. Benny said it was sometimes that way when he did his route early; it would be so windy that his eyes would tear, and then the tears would freeze on his cheeks. But when the pocket warmer got going, it was too hot. Benny said someday I could take over his route.

"Listen," continued the driver, "why don't you let me take that piece apart for you? I'll bet the stock comes—"

"I know! I can do it." Benny wouldn't let the driver touch the shotgun. He snapped it open at its elbow and jiggled with it for a minute. The wooden part came away from the barrel.

The driver said he was glad we'd worked it out, but Benny said, "You mean you're glad you got your own way." Then we sat on the bus with our khaki bags and orange hats and Benny's broken-down shotgun. It was ten o'clock, according to Benny's watch, which still ran pretty well. Keney Cove would be the last stop.

Benny was older than me and bigger, and he showed me how to do things. One time we tried hiking to Bradley Field, thinking to hitch a ride on one of those private planes. Instead, we ended up seeing the inside of the Windsor Locks Police Station. I couldn't keep walking. I got so tired I decided to sit down along the road and stick out my thumb. A man picked me up. He was an off-duty cop. He stopped for Benny, too, when we caught up with him down the highway. Benny said to him, "Why don't you mind your own business?" So instead of taking us to the airport, he took us to the police station.

Benny didn't get angry at me for sticking out my thumb. He joked about it later, after his mom drove out from Hartford and rescued us. Benny's mom didn't think it was a joking matter. "He's just twelve years old," she said, meaning me. "It's up to you to keep an eye out for him." Benny's mom looked like Andy Devine on television, and I wasn't used to her being sore and yelling. I was used to her handing us chocolate candy and letting us do whatever we pleased. She let Benny have all kinds of things, so long as he earned the money himself. He even had a genuine World War II bayonet with real blood stains on it. But this time she went on and on about my being just twelve and how if either of us boys had a father to look after us we wouldn't get into trouble like that.

If either of us had a father to look after us, we probably wouldn't need to take the bus to go hunting in Keney Cove. I had never gone hunting before, but Benny had. His shotgun had checker-patterned carvings on the wood. Benny bought it with money from his route. He got it at Sears.

Benny had the hunting permit, but he said once we got into the woods, I could shoot. I was looking forward to that, firing a real gun. Benny warned me that it would kick, but I knew I could stand it. I'd seen it plenty of times before on television.

Benny was pretty sure we'd find something to hunt. You got to hunt squirrels, rabbits, quails, pheasants—things like that. And it was perfectly okay; you wouldn't get into any trouble, so long as you didn't shoot more than the limit. We had a little booklet that told the limits. I thought it would be fine if we hunted a pheasant or two. Two would be best, one for each of our moms. I asked Benny if he'd ever tasted a pheasant, but he hadn't. He thought it probably tasted like chicken but better because you hunted for it. I could picture handing the bird to mom and seeing her smile and slide it into the oven. Benny explained that you had to pluck a pheasant first, then clean out its guts, and sometimes you had to pick the shot out of it. I figured that two rabbits might be less trouble than pheasants.

When the bus reached the end of the line, we were alone with the driver. As we went out the door, I made a fart sound. Benny laughed and said that was pretty good. He said he hoped there was a different driver on the bus when we were ready to go home.

Keney Cove is a flooded-over bend in the Connecticut River. Woods creep right up to the water, which looked as still as ice, as though it were thinking about being ice. As you walked down along the bank, you could see fields behind the woods, fields of snow in the winter, but corn fields or shade tobacco all summer long. Benny said they grow cigar tobacco out here, the best in the world. My dad had smoked big cigars before he died. Benny didn't know if his dad did or not. He didn't care either. His dad and mom couldn't get along, and his dad left them when Benny was only two. He doesn't remember things about his dad.

Here and there the ground was marshy, and my shoes got wet. I was walking on the inside, closer to the water. Benny walked with the gun slung across his chest pointing away from the water and me. Benny was careful where he pointed it, even when it wasn't loaded.

When we got far enough into the woods so that we couldn't see the bus stop behind us anymore, we decided to try out the shotgun. Benny had ten shells in his bag. He took off his glove and loaded one in. I took off my glove, too, and he let me hold another. It was longer than my thumb and made out of green plastic formed into a tube for the shot and powder.

There was a metal cap that read "Remington Peters 16 GA." I thought that meant they were made in Georgia. Benny said, "Could be."

He pointed to a clump of branches about twenty feet away and said to imagine that's the bus driver. I pictured him standing there in that green jacket, with his thumbs in his belt. Benny shot. A bunch of shredded leaves fell to the ground. Neat! I asked if I could try. He said okay but only once; we wanted to save our ammo for hunting.

Benny loaded it for me and showed me how to hold it. I kept the butt firm against my shoulder and sighted with the bead up front. It was hard to keep both eyes open. Benny said to get him in the head, so I aimed right between where the eyes would be and I hit him. Blam! I stood against the kick, and Benny said, "Frankie, you're a natural."

After the shots, everything sounded especially quiet. Benny said we'd have to go off a ways because the noise probably scared off the animals. We decided to sit down and eat the sandwiches that his mom had fixed for us. That way we'd give the animals some time to get over it and come back.

Benny's mom worked at the diner near Aetna on Farmington Avenue. Sometimes she worked at night. She was a cook, which is maybe why she and Benny are both so big. My mom taught people how to dance at the Arthur Murray studio. She also sold Compton's Encyclopedia door to door. Compared to Benny's mom, mine was thin. She was a lot younger, too. But I doubt that she'd ever let *me* have a shotgun.

When we started out again, Benny explained that we had to be quiet. He showed me how to walk like an Indian. I kept my eyes on the tree branches, looking for squirrels and quails, but I didn't see anything but blue sky through the branches. My feet felt cold. I could see a field through the trees on higher ground away from the river. It looked sunny and warmer over there, and Benny agreed we should hunt there after I told him a few times that my feet were freezing.

In the field, yellow cornstalks, chopped to the height of my knees, broke through the snow crust. They threw shadows that looked golden and warm onto the snow. There was no way you could walk without crunching though. We just crunched into the field, and the sun on my face felt good. Benny said there might be pheasant in a place like this. I kept my eyes open for pheasants.

We didn't go far before we saw some other hunters. Four men walking side by side slowly crossed the field ahead of Benny and me. They saw us and stood still, waiting for us to get close. I said to Benny that maybe they'd let us hunt with them. Benny just laughed as though he doubted it. He said they'd probably tell us to keep the hell out of their way.

"You boys fire those two shots before?" asked a tall man wearing yellow-tinted sunglasses.

"Seen anything?" asked another, a guy with a funny mustache.

"Could we hunt with you for a while?" I asked.

The man with the mustache said sure, just so long as we both stayed plunk in the middle and Benny kept the barrel pointing downrange.

"We know how to hunt," said Benny.

"And you boys keep real quiet, too. If you see anything, just give a little whistle."

I figured for certain we'd get something now.

The men fanned out on both sides of us, and we stalked across the field. Benny shushed me before I could ask a single question. All the guns were pointed forward. I wished I had one.

"Look at her go!" one of the men shouted. "Yee ha!" Four shotgun blasts ripped down the silent field. There, maybe fifty yards ahead, a big rabbit on the run flipped, tail over head.

"Hey, nice shooting!" one of the men yelled.

Benny hadn't even raised his gun to aim.

The men made it over to the rabbit before we did. They were chuckling, and one man, the one in the yellow glasses, held it up by the ears. "You boys want a little hunting trophy?"

I held open the wide mouth of the khaki bag on Benny's

back, and the men dropped the rabbit in. I told them we'd go home and stuff it. "Certainly has enough holes to stuff it through," said the man.

Benny and I headed back, and the four men went on without us. They were passing a flask and joking around. I couldn't believe they let us have that rabbit. "Isn't that something!" I said to Benny.

As we headed back to the river, Benny let me carry the gun. It felt heavy after a while, and we sat down on a log that was soft but a little wet from rotting.

"Let's look at the rabbit," I said.

Benny took off his pack, and we dumped the rabbit onto the dirt. The fur was smeared with smelly brown doo. So were the rest of the shells. It was coming from the rabbit's behind. The rabbit's behind had been blasted open. There was blood, too. Maybe the rabbit had been sick to begin with. It looked bad.

"No wonder they were laughing about it," said Benny. "No wonder they gave it to us."

He sounded disgusted.

"Some present," he said. "Some big deal."

We didn't want the rabbit after that. I thought we should bury it, but Benny just gave it a good kick. We went on. I still had the shotgun.

We reached the river bank and walked beside the current, which was so slow we couldn't hear it running. The mud made the footing slippery, and I was careful holding the gun. I kept an eye out for anything moving besides the dried, brown leaves rustling in the branches.

Then I saw it. A little gray cat running along the ground. Benny told me to swing the barrel up for a shot, but when I pulled the trigger nothing happened.

It wasn't loaded. I asked Benny how come, and he said he'd wanted to be extra careful back there with those men.

"Careful?" I asked. "About what?"

"It was getting crowded back there, that's all."

Then I asked if it was okay to hunt cats. He said he didn't remember seeing anything about cats in the booklet.

"Maybe that means there's no limit," I said.

"Yeah," said Benny, handing over a shell. The cat had gone up a tree. Benny said to be patient. I circled the tree and spotted it halfway up. I aimed along the bead and kept the butt in tight. When I squeezed the trigger, the little cat flew off the tree and hit the ground with a thud.

It lay there quiet and peaceful, with just a little blood showing. The fur was smooth and soft. One of the rear legs had gotten shot off, but I figured we could stuff it anyway. We put the cat into the khaki bag. Benny told me again that I was a real natural.

We didn't have to wait long this time before a bus came. It was a different driver, and he didn't say anything about Benny's gun. He asked if we'd gotten anything, and I told him what.

He looked down at me from his seat at the wheel, and his eyes went suddenly tired. He was an old guy with gray in his hair and crinkles around his eyes.

"That's a hell of a thing to shoot," he said.

"What's it to you?" Benny said.

"People live around here," he said. "Some little boy—"

"It was wild," said Benny.

"Yeah," I said. "It was wild."

We sat down. The door closed with a hiss, and the bus pulled out.

"How do you know it was wild?" I asked Benny.

"Nobody who has any feeling for a cat is going to let him roam wild in the woods all day," he said.

We didn't talk much for the rest of the ride. I was happy just to be warm once again. And I was tired. When we got to our stop, the driver looked away as we walked by him to get off.

"It was wild, pop," said Benny. "Wild."

Benny's mom wasn't at home. The note said there was food on the stove and pie in the oven.

We had some pie, then took the khaki bag into Benny's room. We spread the business section out on the floor and dumped out the cat. I took it by a paw and carried it to the bathroom and ran it under the faucet. The water streamed nicely through the fur, rinsing off the crud that had stuck to it from being in Benny's bag.

Benny said we'd have to clean out the cat's guts. You couldn't just leave it the way it was because it would go hard and stink. Benny had a biology kit, the kind that comes with dead frogs, and he got out the fancy knife with the razor-sharp blade. We took a piece of board and stretched the cat out on it, nailing its three good feet. With the sharp tip of the blade, Benny pierced the cat's belly, right in the middle. He cut straight down to where the cat makes. The thing opened up just like it had been unzipped. The insides smelled musty, like an attic or like your skin smells after they take the cast off your broken arm that's gotten better. Inside the cat's body everything was tucked away as neat as my mother's dresser drawers.

I thought I could tell the heart, but Benny said it was the liver. The heart was under that, inside a membrane, like cellophane. Benny showed me the lungs and the ribs and the stomach and the intestines. It all fit together so neatly. It reminded me of the time we took my watch apart to see how it worked. Benny showed me the little flecks of shot.

He began to skin it, peeling the hide away from all the insides. He used the edge of the knife to help it along. It was like taking a kid's jacket off for him. When Benny got to the feet, it was like the jacket had gotten stuck going off inside out. We couldn't get the skin off the feet until Benny sliced them off. Then the skin slipped away just fine.

Benny had trouble with the head, too. The skin wouldn't come off there, either. We didn't know what to do. The knife didn't help. Benny got out his bayonet and just whacked the head off altogether. We couldn't stuff it, but we still had a nice piece of fur.

We had trouble at the other end, too, but after we lopped off the tail, we had a real pelt. The fur was smooth, and when we cut away the three leg parts, you couldn't tell that one leg had been shot off. It really was a nice little pelt.

Benny said we still had to tan it or else it would get stiff. He went looking for his book about stuffing and fixing up animals, and I scraped away the bits of flesh that were still sticking to the inside of the skin. The inside of the fur was sleek and smooth, like the inside of your cheek when you feel it with your tongue.

Benny said that tanning the skin wasn't going to be easy. First, we had to brush away all the dried blood, and then we had to salt down the skin. If we didn't do that, the hairs would come out later. Then we had to boil up some water with alum and borax mixed in. He didn't think they kept any of that stuff around the house, and we didn't find any.

Benny figured the best thing to do would be to brush it off and salt it down and leave it alone for a while. The book said you could leave it packed away in salt for as long as you liked. He thought his mom would help us get the other stuff, the alum and borax.

Benny got his toothbrush to brush off the dried blood, and then we used the salt shaker. Here and there the skin was still damp from the rinsing, and the salt didn't go on well. It felt rough against my fingers inside the fur.

When we got it pretty well salted, Benny wrapped it in the comics. I figured we'd keep it in his freezer until his mom got us that other stuff, but Benny handed it to me and told me to take good care of it. He said it was mine because I had hunted it.

I liked the way Benny looked after me. He was a real friend. But he had a claim on the pelt too, seeing as how it was his gun, and his place, and he'd taken me hunting. But Benny wouldn't take it back. He said, "No, you keep it. This is the way it's supposed to be, to remember your first time."

He could be pretty stubborn. The way we settled it was we unwrapped the pelt, and Benny sliced it with heavy scissors. Then we each took half. I left for home then, walking through a wind so cold it made me cry. I didn't care. I was thinking how proud of me my father would have been.

How to Touch a Bleeding Dog

It begins as nothing, as a blank. A rose light is filtering through the curtains. Rosy and cosy. My blanket is green. My blanket is warm. I am inside. Inside is warm. Outside is the dawn. Outside is cold. Cold day. My arm reaches for a wife who is no longer there.

The stillness is broken by the voice of a neighbor, yelling from the road outside. "The dog! Your dog's been hit!" It's the farmer down the road, keeping farmer's hours. "The dog!"

It's not my dog, but it is my responsibility. It is Beth's dog. I don't even like him, with his nervous habit of soiling the kitchen floor at night. I used to clean up after the dog before Beth came yawning out of our bed, and that was an act of love, but not of the dog. Now it doesn't matter why I clean up. Or whether.

Beth's dog is old and worn. He smells like a man given to thin cigars. Beth found him at the animal shelter. He was the oldest dog there.

I find the dog quivering on his side where he limped from the road. He has come to the garden gate, where the rose bushes bloom. A wound on his leg goes cleanly to the bone, and red stains appear here and there on the dull rug of his coat. He will not stand or budge when I coax him. A thick brown soup flows out of his mouth onto the dirt.

On the telephone, the veterinarian asks me what he looks like, and I say, stupidly, he looks like an old Airedale. He means his wounds. After I describe them, he instructs me to wrap the dog in something warm and rush him over.

I make a mitten of the green blanket and scoop up the dog. The thought of touching his gore puts me off, and I am clumsy. I scoop weeds and clods as well as the dog. The dew on the grass looks cool, but the blood that blossoms on the blanket is warm and sick. He is heavy in my arms and settles without resistance in my car. He is now gravity's dog.

Driving past the unplowed fields toward town, I wonder if

my clumsiness hurt the dog. Would Beth have touched him? The oldest dog in the shelter! It's a wonder that she thought having a dog would help.

The veterinarian helps me bring the dog from the car to the office. We make a sling of the blanket, I at the head. We lay him out on a steel-topped table. I pick weeds and grass from the blanket and don't know what to say.

The veterinarian clears his throat but then says nothing.

"He's my wife's dog," I say. "Actually, he came from the shelter over on High Street. He wasn't working out, really. I was thinking of returning him."

The veterinarian touches a spot below the dog's eye.

"Maybe," I continue, "Maybe if it's going to cost a lot . . ."

"I don't think you have to make that decision," says the veterinarian, who points out that some pupillary response is missing. "He's dying," he says. "It's good you weren't attached to him."

Beth, I remembered, enjoyed taking the dog for rides in the car.

"These breaths," the veterinarian is saying, "are probably his last."

He seems relieved that he needn't bother to act appropriately for the sake of any grief on my part. He asks, "Did he run in the road a lot?"

"Never," I say. "He never ran at all."

"What do you make of that?"

"Beats me," I say, lying. I watch the dog's chest rise and fall. He's already far away and alone. I picture myself running out into the road.

I watch my hand volunteer itself and run its fingers through the nap of his head, which is surprisingly soft. And, with my touch on him, he is suddenly dead.

I walk back to the car and am surprised by how early in the day it still is. Blood is drying on the green blanket in my hand, but it will come off in the wash. The blood on the carpet of the car is out of sight, and I will pretend it isn't there. And then there's the touch. But soon the touch, too, will be gone.

Dos Serpientes

The woman I live with looks over my shoulder as I sit typing and laughs. "Listen *gringo*," she says, "get to the part about sex soon if you want to hold their interest." I am working at the kitchen table, and she has to squeeze past me to reach the refrigerator. She claws ice cubes from the freezer into her glass. "No one is interested in morality anymore except you," she says. "You and the fathers." I watch her make the sign of the cross and then say, "Take my advice: write about sex."

I had been writing about morality, about the obligations artists shoulder, particularly novelists. Does the artist struggle under unique moral burdens?

"What?" asks the woman I live with. "Still writing about that stuff? No one wants to read about concepts. Tell the story about you and Gubitz's wife."

People think that publishing a novel entitles you to a lifetime of mornings chatting with Merv Griffin, to a lifetime of afternoons, evenings, and nights enjoying the sexual favors of fans, fashion models, television personalities, actresses, your best friends' lovers, your best friends themselves . . . of everyone, except possibly your own wife. This is a ridiculous fantasy. For truly productive writers, the most active appendage must be the pen.

"You've left out the *wives* of your best friends," says the woman I live with, recapping the tequila bottle.

I know my own case best. After publishing not one but two novels, both unheralded, both unsuccessful, I live obscurely in the town of Dos Serpientes, seat of the University of South Central New Mexico, famous in copper-mining circles for its department of metallurgical engineering, and home of the country's smallest graduate program in creative and technical writing. That's what brought me here from Tucson five years ago.

I don't visit the campus anymore. I see it from the highway, the tumbleweeds clotting the perimeter fence, the sunlight glinting off the brown tile of the roofs, the adobe decaying and crumbling.

Dos Serpientes. Two serpents. I'd be hard pressed to invent a fictitious name as befitting. The town lies in the valley of the Rio Grande. The soil, eroded from the lava beds on the western plateau, mixes with the irrigation water to produce the nastiest green chili peppers in the entire Southwest. The people of Dos Serpientes—the people of *la raza*—say that the meanness of the chili seeps into their bones, coloring the town with its particular temper, its particular personality. *¡Caliente!* There are many bars here and one church.

No one considers it a university town. Born here, you grow up to work in the copper mines. If not the copper mines, then on the assembly line at the Eluxor plant, making regulators for microwave ovens and classified Air Force radar screens. Otherwise, you don't work at all. Many don't. Many spend their days in indolent and dusty unemployment, remaining at a remove—a willful remove—from the concerns of us *gringos*.

I live here because it gives me peace.

"Liar!" says the woman I live with. "You stay here because it haunts you, the business with Gubitz's wife."

She exaggerates. It doesn't haunt me. It troubles me a little. Yet, she is right. Gubitz *has* been on my mind. Gubitz and the day we drove toward the lava beds.

Gubitz. It would be a challenge to invent a fictitious name for him as well, a name so redolent of discordancy. Gubitz. The name itself can't settle down in peace here in the Southwest.

"And your name is dripping with adobe?" asks my lover, raking more ice cubes with her fingernails.

My name is Smith, as common as clay.

Where is Gubitz now? New York? They came here from New York. And his wife? He was once my close friend, one of a handful of fellow writers baking away at graduate degrees at the university. For over a year, we sat in workshops together, reading and critiquing each other's work. I admired his writing, the understatement, the irony, the simultaneous sadness and comedy. His characters, calling out to us from an unsympathetic and capricious world, inevitably were victims.

In one of his stories, I remember, an old man, alone in the world, shaking in threadbare clothing, dejected, concludes that he has suffered enough and descends onto the track of the Canal Street subway station in lower Manhattan. He plans to electrocute himself on the third rail and let the express hurtling down to the Battery dispose of his poor corpse. But it is his luck that at the crucial moment a power outage becalms the system. The third rail becomes as tame as a park bench and the trains, out of sight between stations, stall in their tracks.

A sign from God? The man resolves to go on living. Hope rekindles inside him. But climbing back onto the platform, he is bitten by a rat, one carrying a mutant form of plague virus, and is left permanently paralyzed. That story was called "Worse than Dead."

Gubitz himself was thin and anemic. His black, woolly hair was receding prematurely, seemingly backing away from the world that fronted him. I see him stooped, shoulders hunched, as though shivering in the cold. I can picture him in an overcoat the color of gruel, with a rabbit fur collar, holding a bulging briefcase. He'd be right at home in a photograph of the Soviet Politburo. He looked like a C.P.A. That such a reedy clarinet could produce such sad and funny jazz—but there you have it. Few writers look like writers.

"That's a stereotype," says the woman I live with. "C.P.A.s look like everyone else."

Gubitz looked like he needed to be set out in the sun. He was an indoorsman, an introvert. Despite living so close to the desert that the long shadows of the chollas and jackrabbits reached nearly to his feet in the evenings, and despite the ridge of mountains that turned as pink as watermelon in the sunsets, he wrote about factories in Brooklyn and high schools on Long Island. In a town rich with the dinner smells of chili rellenos, frijoles, burros, tortillas, and sopapillas, he dreamed

up characters who ate bagels and pizza. He must have hated it
here.

"Everyone hates it here," says my lover.

Everyone hates it here, but another kind of writer would
make better use of the material at hand. I don't even have to
try anymore. The people, the landscape—it all seeps into my
work. Even now, thinking of Gubitz and of this unsettled feeling I can't shake, I search for analogies and find myself remembering Rafael Lobos.

Rafael Lobos has nothing to do with Gubitz. As far as I
know, they never met. Rafael Lobos was a freshman in the
first English class I taught at South Central. He was an Indian
kid from up north, from Tesuque, I think, or Jemez Pueblo.
One day I mentioned that I needed to learn how to use a rifle;
it was important to a story I was working on. Rafael Lobos,
who never spoke during class, approached me afterward. "Do
you have time now?" he asked.

Sitting in the cab of his truck, a half-rusted, green,'58 Ford
pickup, we drove out of town up to the lava beds. He took me
on roads I didn't know existed, first through the chamiso
grass and mesquite, and then higher into the junipers and
scrub pine. It was on one of these roads that I would someday
take Gubitz.

Rafael's conversation as we drove along was limited. "You
think I drink too much," he said. Until that instant, it had
never occurred to me that he drank at all. I looked at him
closely, probably for the first time ever, certainly for the first
time that day, and saw that his eyes were yellowy and dull. His
hands were shaky. I felt a sensation of unreality. He was indeed drunk, but I experienced it as if he had just become
drunk, at that moment. He made *me* feel drunk.

"Why do you drink so much?" I asked.

"It's what all you Anglos think," he said, looking sick. "We
just drink and don't give a shit."

"I didn't think that," I said, beginning to think it.

We pulled over near an arroyo. His rifle, dragged from
under the seat, was a .22, an old, bolt-action, single-shot .22.

Nothing fancy. If you missed, you had to reload, and few coyotes or crows oblige you by waiting around.

Rafael Lobos had plenty of empties in the bed of his truck. We took turns shooting cans and bottles. He never missed. From the moment he had drawn out his rifle, Rafael Lobos had been completely sober and as steady as steel. Had he been drunk only a few moments earlier? It was impossible.

Half an hour was long enough for me to get a feeling for the way the wooden stock warms against your cheek and to learn the smell and sounds of firing. A hawk flew overhead. Rafael pointed it out to me, saying, "We don't shoot him."

Back at the truck, I expected him to stow the .22 under the seat and start the engine. Instead, he fished out a slender ramrod and began to clean the rifle. With complete concentration, he fitted cotton patches to the notched tip, dripped on some solvent from a little bottle and pumped the ramrod through the barrel. He replaced each grimy cotton wad with a new patch until one came back clean. He was careful about this business and took his time. I stood by, looking at the lazy clouds in the immense expanse of blue sky and thinking of how much better this kid's writing might be if he took the same pains with it.

"You don't let your rifle get crudded," he said. "You get dirt in the barrel, the rifle might blow up in your face."

He passed me the rifle, its bolt removed, and told me to have a look. I raised the muzzle to my eye, as though about to shoot myself, and sighted through the barrel. The rifling inside shone like silver railroad tracks spiraling into the light.

Somehow this image has to do with Gubitz and me. Maybe a writer has to work at keeping his vision unclogged, free of self-deceptions and lies. Maybe that's the writer's moral obligation. Let him screw up his private life; he still has an obligation to keep the line of his vision uncongested.

"Don't make a lecture," says the woman I live with.

Rafael Lobos offered to teach me other things besides how to use a rifle. Was I interested in hawks? In the wind? In potent herbs, as he put it? I felt him looking at me as he drove the truck down toward town. Was he drunk? Sober? I didn't know how to take him. He was too chimerical for me. I never took him up on any of it.

"What does this have to do with the wife?" asks the woman I live with.

Gubitz had a wife. I was dimly aware of this months before I met her. Gubitz from time to time had referred to her, and she had left phone messages for him on our one telephone in the teaching assistants' office. Her voice on the phone, her New York harshness, had sparked an image in my mind.

She would be tense and thin, dressed in unfashionable browns and grays. Her hair would be as lusterless as black beans, worn in a shaggy, complicated braid that somehow brought to mind begrimed Mexican pastry. Her eyes, dark and moist, would bug out with nervous intelligence.

At a department party, one of those endless, joyless affairs seemingly designed to make everyone meditate upon the university's alcohol ban, I first saw her. She was at Gubitz's side, but I should have known her anywhere. She was exactly as I had pictured.

Being on target made me resent her; I would rather have been wrong. Sometimes being right makes the world grow small, so small it begins to pinch. I knew I would never like her.

Gubitz went out of his way to introduce us. She said, "Oh, you're the one who jogs." That was true. I spent an hour a day on the dusty streets leading through and out of town. That's when I did some of my best writing.

"I've been looking for someone to run with," she went on. She explained that running unaccompanied scared her, especially when the boys and men leaning in the shadows behind buildings and in alleyways whistled and hooted after her. *O mamacita! chi, chi, chi.* I knew what she was talking about. Now and then, I got razzed too. I just ignored it. I looked at it culturally: if Dos Serpientes was a sleepy town, then we *gringos* with our foreign habits were its nightmares. Men, and now women too, nearly naked, charging or gasping along through the streets, impatient, breathless, determined to outstrip persistent, invisible demons. Why were we running? What were we running from? Small wonder the people reacted with hostility.

Gubitz's wife wanted to know if she could do her running with me. Both of them looked up at me with hungry eyes, bullfrog eyes. I wondered why Gubitz himself couldn't take up jogging. He needed the exercise. And it wouldn't have hurt him to peer into the world going on outside his head.

"Sure," I told them. "Anytime." I made further noises about the loneliness of the solitary runner, something I had never actually felt, not for a moment. I'm not a cad; I simply hoped that if we could avoid making specific arrangements just then, the whole matter would blow over and be forgotten in a few days' time.

I was wrong about that. Rather too early the following morning Gubitz telephoned, using as a pretext a trifling question of punctuation, (something about the proper placement of semicolons around closing quotes) the kind of fine point no one ever remembers.

"The semicolon," says the woman I live with, "goes outside closing quotation marks." She has the whole book down cold.

Gubitz then put his wife on the phone. Would I be running today? Yes, I said, but in the afternoon. "The heat makes it more of a challenge, don't you think?" This piece of cruelty failed to dissuade her. She volunteered to bike over to my apartment at three.

"Better make that four-thirty," I said, giving up further struggle.

The transformation into gym shorts and oversized t-shirt revealed no hidden, glamorous side, but Gubitz's wife was no beginner. One look at her well-worn Nikes showed that. We did some warm-ups on the driveway by my car and then started out. I hoped that she could match my pace.

I'm not a fast jogger. I go for long, slow distance and rarely break a nine-minute mile. Even so, Gubitz's wife lagged behind. Turning back to say something, I discovered that she ran with a limp. I hadn't noticed it before, but then, she had bicycled over. Seeing her galumphing along like something wounded pained me. But her motions, with an off-beat rhythm of their own, were also fascinating. She was a slightly broken machine: the flywheel still turned at the usual, even rate, but one or two random cogs were missing, and the action pulled and jerked.

Gubitz's wife evidently didn't care how she looked or what anyone thought of it. She was determined to get her running in, obstacles notwithstanding. She must have sensed how little I wanted her tagging behind, and I'm sure she could have imagined a more sympathetic companion. Still, she was willing to put up with me. I began to admire her. I slowed the pace.

"Why don't you write that you began to desire her?" asks the woman I live with.

I did not begin to desire her, but jogging with a woman is sometimes as intimate as lying in bed with her. Your bodies are so close you can smell each other. You can't hide your sweat, your straining breaths, your pain, your indigestion. Every runner sometimes has gas. You spit up phlegm. You belch. And you have no covers to hide under, no lights to switch off. You quickly stand, or shuffle along, revealed. You don't long remain strangers.

Not strangely then, I learned that first day how she had ruined her leg. We had been exhausting the small talk of jogging—how many years we had been running, how many miles a week, how much we had paid for our Nikes—and I asked if she'd injured her leg running. Yes, she said, she had been running—running for her life. She had been attacked on a subway platform. She had kicked and screamed, but no one had helped her. Her calf and knee had been slashed, the worst of the wounds that showed, as she said.

Afterward, she had persuaded Gubitz to come out to Dos Serpientes, even though he had been offered an assistantship at N.Y.U. She couldn't feel safe in New York anymore, that was all. She still at times suffered attacks of panic. That was why she couldn't go running alone, not with those men leaning in the shadows, calling after her.

That was the beginning of it. We ran together almost every day, sometimes talking, often in silence. But after only a few weeks, we conversed without pause, and the runs lengthened from three and four miles to more than five and six. We talked about swamp coolers, Chicanos, Toney Anaya's campaign, teaching, shopping in Dos Serpientes for horseradish, and dieting. I stopped thinking of her as Gubitz's wife and began thinking of her as Myra Gubitz.

Gubitz and I saw each other on campus still, and once they invited me to their place for dinner. We went to see a film together down in Las Cruces. I was soon spending more time with her than with him. I spent more time with her than with anyone.

We—Myra and I—talked about Gubitz. It would have been unnatural not to. After hearing me gripe about spending an entire Saturday grading freshmen essays, she might remark that Allan—that was Gubitz's name, Allan—complained about it, too. If I remarked that the fiction workshop had come down hard on so-and-so's piece, she might say that Allan had really hated the story.

But there was a boundary line running through the topic of Gubitz, and we began to make forays across it. We started speaking of him as though *he* was the outsider. Myra revealed confidences. It made me uncomfortable.

It began with some questions about my being "an unsuccessful writer," as she put it. "Do you send your work to editors?" she asked. I did. "Don't you get a lot of rejections?" In those days, I got rejection slips exclusively. I had them stuffed into the bottom drawer of my desk, thinking that someday they'd make some ironic point.

"But you're laughing about it," she said. "Don't you get depressed?" I got depressed, certainly, but I got over it fast. You develop an immunity to it.

"Allan hasn't," she said. "He sulks for days and days. I

mean days and days. I can't speak to him. He won't eat. He pores over his manuscript searching for the flaw. And then he starts rewriting it. He gets obsessed. I lose him. I hate seeing those manila envelopes come back in the mail."

Once she started complaining about him, there was no turning back. First of all, he blamed her for their having to live in Dos Serpientes. He never said anything so direct, but she could tell that he blamed her. If only he were in the program at N.Y.U., he'd say and then say nothing more. She also told me how jealous he was of the other writers in our graduate program, hating to hear that anyone placed a story, even in the most obscure quarterly like *Sonoran Desert Review* or *Pig Pen*. "Thank God so few of you get published at all," she said. "It drives him nuts." She told me he was comfortable with me because I didn't get published either. "He says you never will," she revealed. "He thinks he's by far the better writer."

I wasn't surprised that Gubitz thought of himself as the better writer. Most of the writers in the program believed that they had more talent than all the others. At least that was true of the male writers. Perhaps that fund of ego, of arrogance, is necessary, like fat on a bear. In my case, I never assumed I was the best writer. In fact, I had plenty of doubts. Dry spells do that to you. Even rereading the material of a year or even of six months ago can do it. You convince yourself that you've lost the spark, certain that you'll never write as well again.

But I was confident that my life was unfolding as it should. Every life has its timetable, its destiny. You never see it directly, but you might have a sense for it. I always had a good sense for mine and tried to go with the grain. I've been off the track a number of times, of course, but never for very long.

So I felt I belonged in Dos Serpientes, struggling with my first novel. Eventually, I sensed, some muse of the desert would take an interest in me, and that has been borne out.

"You aren't being overconfident?" asks the woman I live with.

Of course, I didn't suspect that the muse would be such a nag.

"*¡Chingada!*"

Myra ventilated other complaints about Gubitz. She described his childhood and brought to life before me his overbearing, oversolicitous mother, a figure still on the prowl in Gubitz's life. She hinted at sexual problems, making it clear that they were not so much theirs as his. Things had changed for them once they moved out of New York. She asked if I thought he needed a therapist. And did I think it was wrong to snatch a rejected manuscript from the mailbox before he had seen it and keep it hidden for weeks?

Our disloyal conversations were, nevertheless, satisfying. And we didn't always talk about him. Myra's openness made it easy for me to be open with her. She and I grew as comfortable together as two old shoes.

Our runs began and ended outside my apartment, on the street. It was understood that she would not come inside, but we often took a breather at a spot near the end of a foot trail outside of town in the scrub. There were some boulders and outcroppings to sit on while talking or gazing at the mountain ranges in the far distance. One day, sitting by those rocks, sweaty and relaxed, we stopped talking and just stared at each other. She smiled in a winning, easy way that looked dopey, the way a big floppy dog I once had used to smile at me sometimes. That dog really loved me. I wondered how I had missed seeing Myra's beauty. I wanted to touch her. I wanted to trace my finger down the ridge of red scar that snaked along her knee.

This eruption of feelings frightened me. I wanted to suppress it and realized that for weeks now I had been squelching fantasies involving Myra and me. I never let these fantasies run their course. Gubitz, after all, was my friend, my colleague. How easily I could picture him distressed and brokenhearted. His vulnerability was so apparent that I had trouble remembering that there was much more to him. And I could easily put myself in his shoes.

That day, sitting by the rocks, I revealed nothing to Myra

about my feelings and what had flashed between us. She also said nothing. I was afraid to ask what she was thinking. We jogged home in silence.

The next day, I telephoned early, saying I had developed a pain in my knee. Best to rest it for a while. She was sorry. She didn't question me closely. I said I hoped she'd feel safe jogging alone on those trails out of town. She said she'd give it a try.

And I would give myself time to think. At the office after lunch, I found Gubitz at his desk, pale, unhealthy looking, lost in paperwork. I had become increasingly reserved with him, and now I felt a guilty sense of betrayal. Lately, he had been confiding in a few of us that the editors of a really prestigious literary quarterly had been keeping a piece of his for months. Months. That could be a good sign, he pointed out. It was hard to listen and pretend admiration knowing the exact kitchen drawer into which Myra had stuffed the returned manuscript weeks earlier.

I decided it was time we talked. We needed to clear the air, to find new footing for our friendship. *Listen, Allan*, I planned to say, *I'm talking as a friend. I don't think you realize how unhappy Myra is* . . . After that, it would be up to him. Maybe they'd patch things up, maybe they wouldn't. But I'd feel that I'd done the right thing by them both, the kind thing.

I sat at the edge of Gubitz's desktop. "I won't be jogging for a while," I said.

"I heard about your knee," he said. Of course, she had mentioned my call to him. It hadn't occurred to me to wonder what she told him about our time together. I hadn't really pictured her talking to him about me at all.

"What about a drive up to the lava beds later in the afternoon," I asked him. The lava beds were so primal to the land we lived in, so much literally a part of the bedrock of our lives, that I thought he'd be pleased to get a look at them. He and Myra didn't have a car, and even if they did he might never have gone up there. I suppose I really wanted to get down to the bedrock of our tangled relationships as well. Neither of us taught in the late afternoon, and I knew he didn't have a class then either.

He tried to put me off, saying he needed to get some writing done. I realized that during the time Myra was out of the house jogging with me, Gubitz had made use of the solitude to write. Their apartment was no bigger than the little hole I live in now, and I'll bet it was a relief to get that hour or so every day of total quiet.

"Are you implying that I get on your nerves?" asks the woman I live with. No, I tell her, but it's hard to compose when the sound of soap operas intrudes insidiously day after day. I think she's got me writing soap operas now. What will Smith really say to Gubitz when they drive out to the lava beds? What will Gubitz do when he discovers his wife's secret? What does Myra Gubitz really want? Tune in tomorrow for the continuing story "Dos Serpientes."

Gubitz did finally agree to accompany me, and I picked him up on campus around four o'clock. We drove out of town, leaving behind the last building, the last billboard, the last dusty lot with its dog and ragged children and rusty car sitting up on blocks. We went out among the mesquite trees and all the scrub grass.

We turned westward onto a two-lane blacktop that twisted gradually onto the plateau. Then I found one of the roads of Rafael Lobos. Nothing except the paved road itself hinted of human presence. I expected to see coyote, certainly some rabbits, and possibly—once we gained some altitude—the tail of a stubby mule deer. I looked in the sky and saw Rafael Lobos's hawk.

"Notice anything unusual about this road?" I asked Gubitz, remembering Henry James's remark that a writer is someone upon whom nothing is wasted.

"It's not the Long Island Expressway," he said.

"No electric wires," I pointed out. "No telephone poles. Nothing gives away the year. We could just as well be driving in 1935."

"What if we break down?" he asked.

"I've got a canteen in the trunk somewhere."

"I can't believe how empty it is out here," he said. "There's nothing here."

That reminded me of something a guy, a young *vato*, had shouted at me when I jogged past the door of the bar next to Mi Casita. "What you running from? There's nothing!"

The Toyota was taking the curves well, turning up a new horizon every few minutes. I was pushing seventy miles an hour and feeling the sense of release I get when I'm completely away from traffic. It's good for the engine really to open up once in a while—burns the carbon off the rings. Driving up there does something similar to me.

We started passing snakes. It could have been the elevation or the time of day, but the asphalt must have been warmer than the surrounding dust, and we sped past half a dozen big ones stretched lazily out on the roadway. It was hard to tell whether they were still alive, particularly given our speed and the way I was weaving to avoid crushing them.

As we came around a curve, there lay a bright pink, obscene sinew of snake. I had never seen anything like it before. We were well beyond it when I brought the car to a standstill. I jerked the gears into reverse to go back for a closer look. It was as thick as a phallus and more than six feet long.

With care, I positioned the Toyota to give Gubitz the first close look. The snake lay directly below his side window. He needed only lean out and there it would be, coiling slowly not three feet below him.

I watched Gubitz's fist on the seat beside me. It grew tense and turned white. His body shifted slightly, as though a shudder had coursed through him. Then, making some pathetic bird noise, he shrank violently back from the window. He pressed against me, and I thought I could feel the contractions of his heart. In panic, he rolled his window shut. "Let's go back now," he said.

The snake slithered off the road into the bushes, and we headed back to town. Gubitz said nothing, and neither did I.

He kept that window rolled shut during the journey back. The impulse to tell him everything and to set matters straight had left me. In fact, it struck me as a wasteful gesture.

A week later in my apartment, I held Myra in my arms. "You mustn't live a lie," I told her. I cradled her black hair against my chest, and it smelled like dust. "You deserve more than this," I said.

"This isn't right," she said. I reminded her that she was not someone to let obstacles stand in her way. I said other things; my intuitions were clear. She cried, but she stayed that night.

She stayed for several nights. We had to drive out to Zodys Discount Department Store to get some clothing for her to change into. She was upset most of the time and helpless. I sent out for pizzas, but she wouldn't eat. Life became hellish. Gubitz stopped showing up for his classes, and Myra was sure that he would kill himself. Gubitz's mother called my apartment repeatedly from New York, and Myra insisted on speaking to her every time, even though the conversations left her in tears. Everyone in the department sympathized with Gubitz and ostracized me, treating me as though I were the heartless one.

I felt justified without being able to justify anything. I had done what had felt right.

The world turned topsy-turvy. Myra went away, back to her parents' home back East. She didn't love me. I see now that she didn't need me in the way I thought. It's funny to think of the things you can mistake for love. She had no one else to turn to in this desert town.

Gubitz dropped out of the program altogether, leaving his grade book and course notes in the hands of one of the senior faculty members who mercifully consented to take over the class. If Gubitz ever reconciled things with Myra, I haven't heard about it. I like to think they're together, if only because it became clear to me in the end that she wanted him. I understand he finished his degree at N.Y.U. and has a book coming out with Alfred Knopf, a very good house.

"That's it?" asks the woman I live with. "That's all? Because you think your friend is a coward, you try to take his wife and call it justice? What *machismo!*"

It isn't justice. I've tried to look at it that way and half a dozen other ways, but it never washes. I look down the barrel of my life and there it all sits, that clot that the light can't worm past. It doesn't wash, and won't until I recognize what I should have felt at the time. When Gubitz pressed against me and leaned away from the lush, pink snake in the road, another snake darting across my heart moved out to meet him.

A Member of the Class

And then, to add insult to injury, she strode off after they had stopped for a light, telling him to park the car himself. He was exhausted already, after shuttling from the Zodys to the Zayres, from the Zayres to Sperry's Discount House, arguing over the price of a rubberized, plastic bath mat. Sperry's, at $3.98, was cheap, but didn't she understand that they could live without a bath mat? Only $17.00 remained in the checking account, and the collection agency was already after them about the credit card.

No wonder she had called him a failure. He was only twenty-seven years old. It was an awfully hot morning. He hadn't been sleeping well. He didn't know how he would scrape together money for this month's rent, and he was still fifty dollars in arrears for last month's.

Jerry drove around the downtown plaza three times looking for a parking space. The streets were jammed with shoppers and tourists. Even the side streets were filled. He got stuck in a line of cars and started to perspire. He switched on the car radio, and it worked for a change. But the volume was almost too loud to bear. He would have to get the radio repaired someday. A woman's voice came over the air, purring into distortion. She invited him to buy a home in Casa Rica, in the foothills. A man's voice added that Casa Rica homes start in the low nineties. Jerry pictured drivers all over Tucson listening to the same station and deliberating whether or not they wanted to put down the $90,000. He wanted to switch stations but didn't dare risk losing the signal altogether.

The traffic started to move, and Jerry drove farther and farther out, but so many cars were on the road that he had trouble even changing lanes. When he saw a lot with a few spaces, he pulled in. It was a car dealership, a Ford dealership. That was all right; he was driving a Ford. It was rusting and crumpled along one side, but it wouldn't draw much attention to itself, he hoped.

The new cars in the lot were parked in rows at an angle to the street. They were crowded together tightly, and he would have to back in carefully around the rows to get into a space. He would be grateful once he got out of the hot car. His shirt was wet against his chest. Watching his rearview mirror, he steered a wide backwards turn. There was a tight squeeze on one side, and he concentrated on making it.

Some impulse made him turn in his seat and look directly back through the rear window, and he jammed on his brakes to avoid scraping a brown compact he hadn't even seen. His car lurched to a halt. He would have to be more careful.

Finally settled into a space, he switched off the radio, pocketed his keys, and walked in the direction of the showroom. He thought he would look at the new cars for a few minutes and then walk off to find his wife. He wasn't at all interested in cars, and his ears were still buzzing from the blare of the radio, but walking off the lot toward the plaza would draw too much attention to *his* car.

Before he reached the dealership doors, a man in a gray business suit emerged from a side door in the building's long stucco wall and approached him.

"Excuse me, sir, but you've nicked one of our cars."

"I did?" Hadn't he hit the brake in time? He hadn't heard a thing—but, then, there was that radio. He felt anxious.

The man in the suit walked him over to the brown compact. Over the rear wheel on the left side were two dents stippled with blue paint. There was no question about it.

With his head down, Jerry followed the man back into the building. The man led him into the service area and began to collect some forms. Jerry knew that the smallest dents could run you hundreds of dollars. *Hundreds.*

The man started writing on a large yellow pad. "Let's see," he said as if to himself, "the rear quarter panel has got to be replaced. The labor alone on that is going to run about seven hours. And then there's the chrome strip . . ."

On an instinct Jerry had trouble recognizing as his own, he interrupted the man and said, "But, you know, that lot out there is poorly designed. I don't see how anyone could park there safely. I don't know—maybe we should just wait and settle it in court."

Jerry didn't have the money to go to court, and he knew he had had no business parking in the dealer's lot. But it seemed right to gamble with the situation.

The man put down his ball-point pen and looked at Jerry with contempt. "That lot was designed by a traffic engineer."

"So what?" said Jerry. "I went to Princeton." It was a stupid thing to say, Jerry knew, but he hoped it was the *right* stupid thing. Let the man think he was prepared to lie his way around anything. Jerry stared at the man in the gray suit with all the belligerence he could muster.

The man looked long and silently at Jerry. He looked down at Jerry's sneakers, so old and worn that even the knotted laces were gray, and up at his shirt, stained with sweat, torn at the pocket. Then he looked away as though he were calculating odds.

"All right, you bum, let's forget the whole thing," he said. "Just get the hell out of here."

Jerry didn't waste any time going back to his car. He glanced down at his newest dent, a mild dimple scratched down to the bare metal. He could live with it. It was nothing.

He was glad he didn't have to back the car anywhere to leave the lot. Waiting for an opening in traffic, he decided to turn left, away from the plaza. He realized he was going to celebrate his escape with a beer at the Thirtieth Street Café, a cold, brown bottle of beer served in a frosted glass. Let his wife wait. He could go on for at least another day. Thank God he had gone to Princeton, he thought. He doubted that he could have come up with anything so improbable and unconvincing on his own.

The Death of Rodney Snee

I last saw Rodney Snee alive when Miss Chicoree sent him to the principal's office for calling her a bitch. He was out the door before you knew it. That was his way: fleet, always running. It was sixth period, social studies, and late in the day. The air was heavy with chalk dust. Old Chicoree had been going on about young Teddy Roosevelt, "a New Yorker like yourselves," who had built himself up from a frail and asthmatic little worm (like Neil Jacoby) into an American president. What will power! Determination! Grit! But then Rodney Snee started piping up about the Roosevelts' having millions of dollars, too, and you should see their house, and after all, didn't that money make a little will power go a lot farther?

Old Hickory didn't like to be interrupted or contradicted. No doubt we'd have a sermon about the students of twenty years ago and how, compared to them, we were all this-and-that. Even Neil Jacoby, you'd have to suppose, even creepy Neil with his Theory-of-Relativity science fair project was as unimpressive as a broken stick-ball bat compared with the students who used to go so winningly to this place. But Rodney went on saying, "What does it matter, you old bitch?" That was really asking for it. She didn't holler. She used that whisper of hers that's supposed to herald the end of the world, and she sent him down. That was the last I saw of him, slipping out the door.

Chicoree took the opportunity to threaten the rest of us with our school records. She pressed her knobby and arthritic hands together on the broad surface of her big wooden desk and stared right at me. Why me? She looked like a hawk, even with the blue rinse that made her hair look a poodle's.

"Edward," she said, "Can you define the word *foredoom* for the benefit of your peers?"

Old Hickory was very nice about vocabulary and often tried to catch me up because I scored high on the STEP test.

"It means ruined in advance," I said, too wary to say either *hell* or *damned* in front of her.

She got up from her desk, aching and creaking, and moved to the corner of the room by the flag. "In the vault behind the main office stands the records file, as you know. There's a card for every person in this room. Someday when you apply for a job or seek entry into a college, that card from P.S. 177 will accompany your application. The black marks you've made on your records here will follow you throughout life. You, too, can be ruined in advance."

She gave us a significant pause.

"Think about that."

I didn't want to think about that. Sitting two rows over, as a reminder, was Franny Phlotz. Certainly a black mark on my record. One day two years ago I was summoned to the principal's office for pelting her with snowballs all the way home from school (three blocks). Why did we have to live next door to her? It still bothers me to think of all the mornings we spent playing with Lincoln Logs on the rug of her living room. I had been too young to know better. And then her crying in the principal's office. "He hurt me! I have no friends! I hate it, I hate it, I hate it!"

And everyone wanted me to explain why. Why, why, why! I didn't know why. It was just the way things were. Fat Franny. I said, "It didn't hurt her," but no one listened. A black mark, no question.

But my record was an angel's compared with Rodney Snee's. Poor Rodney! Many were the times I'd have poked his eyes out if I could've gotten my hands on him. He used to call me "Eddie Pancake" because the back of my head is flat. Then everyone started calling me Eddie Pancake. Stinking Rodney was too fast to catch. He'd even go over the schoolyard fence if he had to. One time Richie Boyden helped me to grab him, but even then he slipped away.

"Hey listen," he said, "I was only kidding. You can take a joke, Eddie. You wouldn't hit me, would you, you're bigger than me . . ."

But then, once you'd let him go, he'd just move off ten or twelve feet and start calling you Eddie Pancake again.

Rodney lived somewhere up near Rosie's Store, where you could get firecrackers sometimes and CO_2 tubes. Gangs were supposed to loiter around in that neighborhood, so naturally our parents didn't allow us to go there. Carmine Fuckenafonga came from there, too. They say he lit the fire that destroyed the old Boys' Club. You can imagine his record! He's even got a couple of J. D. cards. Already he's been held back twice, so he's still in the sixth grade (but fortunately not in our class). Nobody can pronounce his name, so we call him Fuckenafonga. Not to his face, though.

I saw him lose a fight only once, and that was with my brother, which is one more reason for avoiding him. We were playing tackle, and he came by and asked for his ball back. He didn't play football (thank God) and, of course, it wasn't his ball. Fuckenafonga didn't expect anyone to stand up to him, though. Fuckenafonga. My brother beat him up. My brother is actually a pretty big guy, especially wearing shoulder pads.

I don't have problems with Fuckenafonga; I just avoid him. Everyone does, if they can. And since he lives over by Rosie's Store, he's easy to avoid. The only time when I can't avoid him is when I work Safety Patrol in Little America, the worst post, three blocks over in their direction. I'm supposed to keep everyone on the curb until the light changes. "OK, you can cross now." "You can't cross yet." "OK, now you can cross."

When Rodney Snee came to the crossing, I used to pretend he wasn't there. On days when Carmine Fuckenafonga comes, when he isn't tardy or truant, I try to pretend that I'm not there. I'd be a fool to try to stop him from crossing, and I'd be a fool to report him, either.

Since he and Rodney both lived back there, you'd think they'd have palled around some. You'd think they'd have had lots to talk about: what to do with your hands when the principal is yelling at you, how to forge absent notes, things like that. What to say when they yelled "Why?" after the evidence was in. But if they walked to school together, I never saw it.

Maybe Rodney was afraid of him, too. And you don't think of Fuckenafonga as having any friends. Of course, it's too late now.

The day old Dickory shook her brittle, twisted finger at Rodney and sent him down to the office was a Friday, and it wasn't until Monday that I heard he got killed. Some of the guys saw it. Richard Boyden said Rodney ran out of the school-yard into the street and got smacked by a dump truck. He said it was a hundred and fifty feet before the driver even real-ized he'd hit something and began to brake. It was stupid of Rodney to run into the street. And at five o'clock when the traffic is always heavy. Normal people don't do things like that. An ambulance came, but he was already dead. You couldn't really see anything because of all the traffic. That's what they said. I wasn't there.

It took about five minutes Monday morning for everyone in the school to hear about it. The principal must have known in advance, because they held an assembly for the whole school and had flowers on the stage. Wednesdays are the usual as-sembly days, and we're supposed to come with ties. Usually you have to sing at the beginning of the assemblies, but we didn't have to this time.

Up front, on the stage with the flags, was a big arrange-ment of flowers, and beside the principal sat Hickory Dickory herself. The principal went first.

"Boys and girls," she said, "I have some very sad news for you today." She went on about Rodney's "sudden and unfor-tunate demise," as if we didn't all already know about it. The flowers, it turned out, were a "gesture of condolence" to the family. (The principal encouraged a big vocabulary, too.)

Then came Miss Chicoree. I was certain she was going to start in again about keeping our records clean. What an op-portunity this would be! Hadn't she told us a million times how badly our lives would turn out if our records were rotten, if we were foredoomed?

Now she had proof. Everyone knew that Rodney would

never have been hired anywhere or gotten into college—not with his record. It was getting scary to think about how these things turned out. A dump truck. And there, two rows in front of me, was the very same, hunchy back of Franny Phlotz that I had so effectively pelted two years before.

But Miss Chicoree mentioned neither records nor black marks. Instead, she started talking about Rodney as though she had liked him.

"We all must feel a sense of sorrow in this lad's death, but I hope and pray that as we go through life we will better be able to understand such tragedy." I started to get fidgety. At any moment I expected her to start shouting "Why? Why, why, why!"

Why, indeed! Why was she covering up for him? Why was she pretending to like him and feel sorry for him? Why did she call it a tragedy? She'd practically predicted it.

I was sitting next to Neil Jacoby, and I asked him, "Is it a tragedy?"

"Naw," he sniveled through his asthma, "he had it coming."

Richie Boyden, who was sitting in the row behind us, whispered "Yeah, but think of the pain."

"Pain doesn't last," Neil pointed out, always the scientist.

"I seen it," said Richie.

A bunch of kids in the lower grades were crying, but they didn't know Rodney. It's easy to get little kids crying, and Hickory's remarks about the "poor fellow whose future was lost" were pretty sad if you didn't know the facts.

What finally brought Hickory's oration to a close was Carmine Fuckenafonga, who had come to school that day, and who was sitting under his pompadour about twenty seats over to my right. Somebody yelled out, "Look, Fuckenafonga's crying!"

I didn't actually see him crying, and I don't think he was. Why would he cry about Rodney Snee? What I did see was him swinging at everyone near him. By the time we all got out of the way, the principal was yelling and clapping, trying to get everyone to settle down and sing "Our Father's God to Thee." After that, the assembly was over. Carmine Fuckenafonga got suspended (as if he cared), and we all went back to class.

Another Thursday with the Meyerhoffs

Meyerhoff perched on his porcelain throne upstairs waiting for the phone to ring and bring in some business. He had the morning paper spread out over his knees. Downstairs the door slammed shut, and a moment later he heard the life jump into the engine of his wife's car, a wide-axled Pontiac the color of martini olives. She was leaving for her Thursday therapy appointment. Meyerhoff's wife had been diagnosed as infertile. The diagnosis had been reconfirmed. They never talked about it now, but she blamed him. She didn't say it in so many words, but he could tell. Meyerhoff couldn't remember whether she had just come up the stairs to say goodbye. She had come up for something—probably to tell him to walk the dog.

His wife was a woman of intense moods. Her therapy hours stirred her so that, when she came back to the house, she invariably retreated into the bedroom to cry. Later she would be ready to face Meyerhoff and the world again, but she never discussed her therapy sessions. She was often resentful of Meyerhoff, though, and even openly hostile. She brought up remarks Meyerhoff had made in all innocence during the previous week and then showed him how insensitive and uncaring he had been all along. On occasion, she returned filled with love for Meyerhoff. Or if not with love, then with sympathy, which Meyerhoff was willing to settle for. Meyerhoff never knew what to expect when his wife came home from therapy, except that she would close the bedroom door and cry.

Meyerhoff's dog was six months old and had developed into a car chaser. Actually, he was Meyerhoff's wife's dog, but Meyerhoff exercised him as frequently as his wife did. More frequently. The dog had some shepherd in him and was shaped like a bullet. When Meyerhoff took him over to the baseball

fields behind Catalina High School, the dog invariably squat-
ted and did his business. But Meyerhoff's wife, who loved the
dog, had many dry runs. Sometimes she would return from a
dismal half-hour of it, her blouse dripping with perspiration
from the midday Arizona sun, and she would shrug. Then
Meyerhoff would get up from his pile of real estate clippings
and take the dog out again. The dog's name was Sunshine,
something Meyerhoff's wife had come up with. Meyerhoff
made the effort not to call him Sunny.

The Meyerhoffs lived blocks away from Speedway and Grant
Boulevard, the heavily trafficked streets. Their neighborhood
with its tall palm trees was quiet, and they didn't put Sunshine on a leash. Sunshine wasn't used to a leash and wouldn't
squat with one on.

Meyerhoff folded his paper and stood up, once again disappointed. There was nothing to see, and he didn't bother to
flush. He washed his hands out of habit. He looked at himself
in the mirror and worked up the smile he used on his clients.
The wrinkles fanning away from his eyes were cut deep into
his face. It was the climate. It was the sun. It was the smile
itself. He worked it up again and saw that he looked fero-
cious, feral, maniacal. It was depressing. He had expected to
see a younger man's face when he looked in the mirror. His life
was . . . what? Not even half over. Meyerhoff noticed that
once again his wife had left the toothpaste uncapped.

Meyerhoff padded down the stairs to collect the dog. He
eased his feet into running sneakers that still looked new after
six months, and the two of them headed through the heat toward the high school.

The first car that came along, the dog went for it, barking
with delight, his claws scratching the hot, graveled surface of
the street. Meyerhoff was too old to chase after the dog. He
might have done it five years ago, but not now, not in public.
Besides, he had a bum leg from a fall while skiing down Mount
Lemmon a few years back. He bellowed at the dog, but the
dog ignored him.

Meyerhoff wished he could deliver a long-range shock to the dog. He wished he had an electrical device attached to the dog's collar. Sunshine pranced back to Meyerhoff after the car got away, but he stayed far enough out of range to escape easily should Meyerhoff make a sudden lunge for him. The dog and Meyerhoff had been through this before.

Sunshine wouldn't sniff up to Meyerhoff's hand even though he held out a dog cookie and made his voice sound friendly. Sunshine knew better. He was a big puppy, and his ears flopped. The ears didn't stand up like a shepherd's ears. Meyerhoff wished he had a little button in his hand that would give Sunshine a handsome surprise.

The dog was no better at home. Sunshine woke Meyerhoff at daybreak with his pathetic whimpering and cold nose. Meyerhoff's wife seemed to encourage the dog in this. His wife was always happy to see the dog in the morning.

Meyerhoff was sure that the dog was jumping on the furniture when he was out. He hadn't caught him at it, but he had found hairs on the blue-and-coffee-colored serape they had bought down in Nogales. Meyerhoff had plans to sneak up to the house some afternoon and peek through the living room windows. He also suspected that his wife let Sunshine sit on the big, leather lounge chair.

Meyerhoff had spent hours training the dog to sit still and to lie down on command, but the dog would do nothing unless bribed with dog cookies. Sometimes not even dog cookies availed. When Meyerhoff's clients—young marrieds, retired couples—came over to look at listings, the dog was incorrigible, barking and snapping. On quiet evenings, the dog liked to visit Meyerhoff's lap the moment he opened his magazine. Sunshine also stationed himself in front of the screen when the television news came on.

Sometimes Meyerhoff got down on the rug to roughhouse with the puppy. Actually, he would pinch the dog with vengeance and hope that his wife didn't notice. He would take up the loose skin on the dog's back and give it a quick bite. Or he would clamp his fist around the dog's snout and hold it until the dog squealed. Meyerhoff would pretend that the puppy had squealed with delight.

Following the dog through the gate into the grounds of the high school, Meyerhoff wished he had the dog's snout in his fist right then. The dog trotted ahead, hurrying to try to spray his latest news on two ornamental mesquite trees and the base of the drinking fountain. But he quickly got down to it on the clay track just in front of the home team's stands.

The dog strutted over to Meyerhoff, grinning, and Meyerhoff scratched behind his ears. He wanted to walk over and inspect the dog's stool but thought better of it. A chubby man jogging the track was eyeing him, and he would have felt silly. At least the dog hadn't started chasing joggers. Meyerhoff's running shoes still looked new because he didn't jog. The chubby man, who was at least Meyerhoff's age, waved to Meyerhoff, but Meyerhoff pretended that he hadn't seen. Meyerhoff didn't like chubby people. He didn't like messy things. He was pleased that he had managed to keep his own weight down without jogging. But then, maybe jogging would be the thing to loosen up his system?

The dog's system didn't need loosening up, Meyerhoff reflected, as he walked homeward past the front yards of his neighbors, yards decorated with saguaros and prickly pear cactus gardens or with bushy oleanders, their pastel flowers scenting the air. It intrigued Meyerhoff that he could always get the dog to squat, but his wife couldn't. The dog just took him more seriously. The dog knew that he, Meyerhoff, could really let him have it, back home on the rug. The dog probably regarded him as the leader of the pack.

They made it home without encountering another car.

Later, Meyerhoff's wife came out of the bedroom, dabbing a wad of pink tissue paper inside the corner of her eyeglasses. She wanted to know if he had taken the dog out.

"Sure," he told her, a little wary. "And he was right on the money."

Meyerhoff's wife moved into the kitchen and started to mix

herself a drink. Meyerhoff went into the kitchen too and leaned against the counter. The dog was in the corner underneath the vent from the swamp cooler. The fan was running at top speed, and they had to raise their voices to hear each other.

"It's no wonder," said Meyerhoff's wife. "He saves it for you."

"What do you mean?" said Meyerhoff. It annoyed him that his wife never offered to mix a drink for him too. Years ago she had served in a cocktail lounge, and she knew how. It wasn't exactly a cocktail lounge, but what else could you call it? She had worked there, and he had been a regular. He had even played softball on a team the place sponsored. It could happen to anyone.

"Don't you ever wonder why the dog holds it for you?" she asked. She had her drink in her hand and was leaning against the counter, too. "Don't you ever wonder?"

"So what?" said Meyerhoff.

"I'd say it was pretty obvious," she said. She held up her glass and stared into it, just as if she were analyzing a urine specimen. "It's the only thing he ever does that pleases you. It's the only thing that either of us does."

The remark took Meyerhoff aback. What if she's right, he wondered. The dog's regularity gave rhythm to the day. It gave the day shape. It did please him. He realized that it did please him. He could admit that. He turned to her and told her that it did please him. And then he worked up one of his smiles.

Off in Zimbabwe

The last time his wife had brought up this business of their sex problems, she had screamed that no way was she going to dress up in Saran Wrap and a purple bow and meet him at the front door.

"That's fine, that's fine," he had said, feeling as bewildered as he did when he came into a movie late. He hadn't understood how cellophane had come into the picture—possibly it was something she had seen on the soaps—but the last thing he needed in the evening was to come home to a woman in a plastic slipcover. "That's not the problem," he had told her.

"What is?" she wanted to know.

He didn't have an answer and could only shrug. And now, two days later, she was coming at him waving her shiny magazine in the air, her ladies' magazine with a movie star smiling pinkly on the cover.

"Listen to this, Frank, okay? It's by a marriage counselor. A *sex* counselor."

Frank had been floating on the living room couch holding the Sunday paper over his head, making a newspaper tent. He would rather have kept reading, but he struck the tent and put his feet on the carpet. The newspaper collapsed into its neat sections, the head of the troublesome Central American junta staring up from page one. He leaned back into the couch and looked up at Sheril, holding the magazine in her two hands as if it were sheet music and she were about to sing. Frank noticed that she had painted her nails maroon. It was Sunday, and they hadn't any plans.

Sheril gave the magazine a little shake and began to read. "'No one doubts that marriage is in trouble today,'" she said, making her voice sound professional, like a disinterested sex counselor's, "'and few are the couples who make it past the crucial seventh year.'" Sheril paused to give Frank a significant look. They had been out to Tia Elena's Mexican Restau-

rant just a month earlier for their second anniversary. Frank
tried to smile. The fingers of his right hand pressed into the
face of the junta strong man at his side.

"'But many married couples,'" Sheril went on, "'can put
the zing back into their lives if only they would learn to communicate effectively about the stresses they face.'" Sheril
went into the divorce rate statistics that came with the article
and then enumerated the typical sources of stress during the
first years of married life.

Frank wondered if any of this were really news to anyone
anymore. Still, he couldn't help ticking off in his head the
stresses that applied to them, to him and Sheril. They had re-
cently moved to a new city. Yes, they had driven out from
Dayton to live in Arizona. But that was six months ago. Now
they knew their way around the El Con Mall and the Park Mall,
and they were no strangers to the Tanque Verde Swap Meet.
They were still talking about going out to the Desert Museum,
and he had even discovered a quiet, hideaway bar on Thirtieth
Street, a place where no one from Ohio or Iowa or Michigan
was likely to walk in under a cowboy hat and want to dance
the two-step.

They had some money worries, too. They were over their
credit limit on the VISA and were still paying off plenty on the
Sears card, not to mention what they still owed Mobil and
Shell. He was new to his job, too, and that was on the magazine's list. But at least they had kept him on the payroll through
the last round of layoffs. Burr-Brown Electronics, Inc.; at least
he wasn't unemployed.

He and Sheril were scoreless when it came to having children, and children, according to the magazine article, were
even more stressful than parental death. Sheril's parents and
his were holding up pretty well it seemed. His mother had
just remarried, and her father had moved down to Fort Lau-
derdale. If any of them were having problems, Frank and
Sheril didn't know about it.

Sheril got to the end of the list, and Frank didn't know what
it all added up to. He could tell that the article held nothing

for him, but he sat attentively, pretending to listen, thinking of other things. His life was pretty comfortable now. He appreciated how comfortable the couch was, for instance, how commodious. He hadn't banked on moving into a new, adobe-styled, stucco townhouse complex and certainly not one nestling a turquoise swimming pool, a Jacuzzi, and a tennis court, but that's how they did things in Arizona it turned out. He and Sheril had driven to the east side, toward the Rincons, with that oddball real estate guy and his nasty puppy, and this is how it had turned out. All he had to do was look out the tinted windows and there they were, other young and healthy couples sunning on lounge chairs right by the pool. Palm trees that still seemed like stage props baked in the heat. Off in the distance, beyond the red tile roof, lay the Santa Catalina mountains, hazy and indifferent.

Their duplex had come with all the extras. Even the air was centrally cooled throughout the complex, so they didn't have to worry about it. Their windows were the kind that didn't open. On the walls, they had hung sections of a cosmetics company's billboard, things Sheril had found down in Nogales and had had framed. Two eye sections were up in the living room, each rich with vermilion shadow and black liner. Two moist, tomato-red lips puffed air on the bedroom wall upstairs. Lately, when they tried to make love, Frank found himself staring at the cosmetics company's lips. Sometimes they began to look like a pair of pulpy worms to him, inching along. Or maybe they were a mother worm and her baby worm.

Sheril wanted to know if he was listening. She wasn't reading to him for her own benefit. She dumped herself into the rattan chair and sipped Tab from a tall tumbler, her maroon fingernails faintly clicking on the glass. Frank realized that her long fingernails bothered him. They were extravagant and vulgar. But that was her business. Her body was her business.

Sheril settled down to read again. "'A couple we know got into trouble because of a communications problem. Skip had always enjoyed initiating oral sex with Sarah, but when she went off the pill and started using a diaphragm, he was put off by the odor of her contraceptive cream. Instead of discussing his feelings with Sarah, Skip kept them to himself. But the frequency of his oral-genital contacts declined and Sarah felt frustrated.'"

"I thought that's supposed to be a family magazine," said Frank. "People like your mother read that magazine."

"Sex isn't dirty, Frank," said Sheril. "Do you think sex is dirty?"

"That's not it," said Frank.

"Then what *is* it?"

Frank didn't know. He had a bad feeling, but it wasn't something he could put into words. Something was wrong though. Something was being ruined. It was as if they were describing sex but meaning tennis. Skip had always enjoyed playing a quick set with Sarah, Frank thought, but then she started developing her backhand. . . . It was wrong.

"Just listen," said Sheril. "'Sarah took her revenge by refusing to perform oral sex with Skip. Although he had always looked forward to and enjoyed fellatio, Skip began to suspect that Sarah had always found it distasteful. Neither Skip nor Sarah communicated their feelings, but their frustrations grew. When they came to us for counseling, Skip was on the verge of an affair with another woman and Sarah was plagued by migraine headaches.'"

Sheril laid the magazine on the coffee table beside her chair and began ransacking its one drawer. She scraped through the plastic poker chips, the packs of playing cards, the expired *TV Guides*, but came up with nothing.

"I'm out," she said.

He had a pack of Winstons in his shirt pocket. She usually smoked a mentholated cigarette, but a Winston would do in a pinch.

"So, what do you think?" she asked, turning away, glancing out the window toward the pool, but then quickly turning back at him.

Her face looked drained. He could see that she was nervous, afraid of what she might hear—afraid, but almost certain of the bad news coming. That's how she looked; Frank knew her looks. At the mall, he knew when she was going to buy something—a blouse, a new bra, some earrings—just from the way she twitched her eyes when she held the thing up to look it over. But this time she was wrong. It wasn't what she was thinking. He wasn't sure what she was thinking, but it wouldn't be that.

The thing was, he was repelled by Skip and Sarah. That was what he thought. They made him want to punch someone or go out and puke. Skip and Sarah added to a bad feeling he had had for weeks. It was as though he had eaten carpet. It was as though a sponge, saturated with mop water, with dirty, chocolate-gray mop water, were churning in his stomach. This feeling came and went, but he felt it when he was up in bed with Sheril.

How had the magazine article phrased it? A couple we know? Yes, Frank thought, he knew them, too. They were living in a neat, white box just like their own apartment. They were probably outside sitting around the pool, Skip and Sarah, catching some sun and giving their busy genitals an airing. Frank wanted to tell Skip and Sarah to try reading a newspaper some time, to try something substantial, not like that ladies magazine or daytime television.

Of course, even Sheril watched the soaps. He had seen her at it, sitting at one of the little, red, foldout trays, watching the tube and playing solitaire. The whole thing had made him feel sad. He had wanted to shout at the people on the screen, "Why don't you stay in your homes and read some books!" No one on television ever reads, he had noticed. Naturally, if they stayed home and read books, they wouldn't get embroiled in so much trouble.

Sheril, still waiting in the rattan chair, was stubbing out her cigarette. "Well?" she said, "What about it?"

"There's nothing wrong with your cream, if that's what you're wondering. You smell like lemons."

"Lemons?"

"Faintly. Subtly. It isn't a problem."

Sheril stared at her hands. "Are you seeing another woman?"

Frank felt sorry for his wife, sorry for what he was putting her through. He detached himself from the grip of the couch and came up behind her, putting his fingers on her bare shoulders. He kissed her neck through the little wisps of hair and pressed his tongue into the spot where she was sometimes salty.

"There's no other woman," he said.

"How come you come home an hour late half the time?" she asked, her voice strained. "You never tell me where you are."

"I do tell you. I go down to the university, to the library. I read the papers there. The New York papers. The Washington papers. I've told you this. What's the big deal? Where do you think I go?"

"I don't know," she said. "To that seedy bar you like so much. Maybe you were meeting someone there."

He was sorry that she didn't understand him better. He was sorry that he didn't understand himself better. But there was no other woman. He used to be drawn to other women, but no more. In fact, he often felt repelled. The women in his division were pleasant and pretty, but they were like office furniture. So were the men.

It made sense that his wife suspected him. Taking a lover was what you were supposed to do when your life went hollow. He didn't need to read a ladies' magazine to know that.

Sheril had the beak of her index finger in her mouth, and it looked as if she might start to gnaw it. His wife was in pain, but Frank couldn't help wondering whether she would get maroon paint caught between her teeth.

"Do you want to go to bed?" he heard himself ask. He hadn't meant to ask that, but it had come out all the same, a balm of well-meaning trying to masquerade as love.

"I want to read something else to you first."

Frank relapsed into the couch, then sat up stiffly to tap out a Winston for himself. Sheril read through a description of a

sensitizing technique, apparently a sidebar to the sex therapist's article. The couple was to lie together naked, but love-
making was expressly forbidden. This was understood in
advance. In fact, directly touching the other's genitals was expressly forbidden, as well. The point was to rediscover the art
of touching, of feeling, of being intimately together. Sheril
wanted to try it.

Frank pictured Skip and Sarah in their own place enjoying
the technique. Sarah would now be rid of the offending sperm-
icide. Skip would be urging his clean and muscular fingers into
the soft pulp of Sarah's bosom, while Sarah would be wanting
him, wanting him to forget their agreement and plunge over
the line, plunge and dart his artful, athletic tongue into her.
Frank pictured them afterward, drawing on their cigarettes,
feeling at peace with the world, thinking about tennis or
switching on Johnny Carson.

Frank left his Sunday paper on the couch and followed
Sheril upstairs. Sheril pulled her yellow tube blouse over her
head, arching her back and freeing her breasts from confine-
ment. Her skin was white and smooth where it wasn't tanned,
and Frank was confronted with her beauty. It struck him how
beautiful and yet anonymous her body was. Plenty of other
women could have the same body. Plenty of other women *did*
have the same body. She had seen to that. They had all seen to
that. She ate cottage cheese and drank Tab and did all the
things Jane Fonda advised her to do. The special Sherilness of
Sheril was something that existed apart from her body.

Frank stepped out of his trousers, and the two of them lay
atop the covers of their bed. Sheril made her fingers into crab
claws, and the crab scuttered over his chest. The maroon nails
definitely put him off, but it was a point of honor not to mention it. Skip would certainly mention it after what he had been
through with Sarah's cream. But not Frank. It was Sheril's
body, after all.

Sheril's crab climbed up close to the edge of Frank's crotch,
nibbling his thighs. It wasn't an unpleasant feeling, but he
wished he felt more.

Then it was his turn. He hovered above his wife's recumbent body and massaged her legs, one after the other. Kneading her skin between thumb and forefinger, he worked his way over her thighs to her stomach. She had closed her eyes and that was a comfort. Her skin felt rubbery and unreal.

"You're going too fast," she complained.

He slowed his hand and settled into a new pace. He started looking at the cosmetics poster. The glistening lips were obscene and unreal. Sheril kept her lipsticks in a neat row in the medicine cabinet. Frank was sure that she had at least a dozen lipsticks. He was working on her breasts now, and he knew how she liked to be touched. Touching her was doing nothing for him, but she seemed to be soothed. He could do it automatically at this point. He had been doing it automatically for weeks.

"What are you thinking about?" she wanted to know. She was staring up at him.

He shrugged. He wondered how long she had had her eyes open. She took his hands off her breasts.

"Tell me."

"I was thinking about Matabeleland," Frank admitted. "They're killing the Ndebeles again. The Shonas—"

"What are you talking about?"

"In Africa," Frank said. "That whole business between Mugabe and the other one. You know, the other one."

"I don't know!" Sheril pushed Frank's body away from hers and sat up against the headboard. She yanked the sheet up and covered herself and then started poking through the drawer in the side table. She was out up here, too.

"Frank, I can't believe this. Our whole goddamn marriage is at stake, and you're off in Africa! Who cares about Africa!"

"It was something I saw in the paper. An Ndebele family was brewing beer outside their hut. Mugabe's soldiers rushed them. Where were the guerrillas hiding, they wanted to know. The family said nothing. The soldiers shoved them into their hut and torched it. Then they started firing—"

"Frank!"

"Only one little girl survived. One girl from an entire village. And her back was nearly burned off."

"What has that got to do with us? They're a million miles from here. You're supposed to be concentrating on my body. You know, we've got problems too."

Frank was staring into the lips on the wall. "This was just last week," he said.

"Give me a cigarette," said Sheril.

Frank got off the bed and found his shirt. Sheril had a butane lighter by her bedside and lit her own cigarette. She blew smoke toward the ceiling, and Frank sat on the edge of the bed.

"I think we better start seeing a therapist," Sheril announced.

"Sure," said Frank, "A therapist." He started thinking about Skip and Sarah and how happy they probably were by now. She was probably back on the pill, but, hey, that's a small price to pay when it comes to giving pleasure. She was probably back on the pill, but as long as he was happy, she was happy. And as long as she was happy, he was happy. Sure.

A therapist, Frank thought. A lot of good a therapist was likely to do. Would the therapist work out his problems with the junta once Africa was squared away? He could already see it in the ladies' magazine. A couple of our acquaintance got into difficulties because they could no longer communicate. Frank, the husband, was off in Zimbabwe, a million miles from here, while Sheril, his wife, complained that they never had fun anymore.

Something was awfully wrong, but he couldn't put his finger on it. Frank looked over at Sheril, still smoking and staring at the ceiling. She didn't know what he was talking about. His world was coming apart, but she was still eager for some good times in it. No, his world had already come apart. That sick feeling started to percolate in Frank's stomach. He pursed his lips together, and they felt wormy. He turned to Sheril, but she drew away from him on the bed.

"Don't touch me," she said.

He hadn't wanted to touch her. He had just remembered the name of the other one, the one fighting Mugabe. Nkomo. He was about to say it was Nkomo, but Frank could see that there was nothing to say. What else was there to say?

Carter

This was at college, and the fellow I shared rooms with was seeing a girl, a young woman, who was beautiful in a particularly quiet way that some women are beautiful, a way that makes you want only to touch her fingers or her waist and never need to say a word. She was quiet like that, perhaps too modest and shy, and she never took the slightest notice of me. I was always just on my way out when he brought her up those five flights of stairs to our rooms in Marquand. That was our arrangement. He would have done the same for me if the occasion arose. I don't begrudge him that. He'd bring her in and take her scarf and coat, and she would look down at Carter's Persian rug, her wool skirt unwrinkled, her crisp blouse neatly fastened at the wrist, her black hair severely cropped and neat. And I would find the door, excuse myself, and plunge into the night. I'd sit through a film at the Brattle or take a lonely stroll beside the Charles. And I'd often wind up at the M.I.T. library, in those days open all night.

His name was Carter, the fellow I lived with, and although she was beautiful and took pains about little things, he never boasted. He took everything with equanimity, as if it all were coming to him. It was confidence. I suppose it was confidence, the main difference between us. I don't mean confidence about courses and exams, but a more fundamental confidence about just being alive. I used to think about this a lot: Carter and me. He wasn't especially handsome. He needed more weight, and he had too much chin. His lips were thin, almost severe. No one would say that he was better looking than I. And I, with my hair sticking straight up like a brush, was as ordinary looking as milk. He was bright and clever in a collegiate way, but so was I. So was everyone. Unlike me, he didn't have a stuttering problem. And he had an air about him, a sureness—something I would never have. That's what drew her to him, I suppose.

I was nervous around women. No, not exactly nervous but solicitous. Are you comfortable? I'd ask. Are you warm enough? Would you want me to open a window? We don't have to see this film if you'd rather see another. Is that chair comfortable? Would you rather have this seat? Can I get you something to eat? A drink? Some wine perhaps? Coffee? Tea? I couldn't imagine a woman being happy with me unless I worked at it, and, of course, I worked too hard at it. But not Carter. He took it all for granted. He never cast a worried glance over his shoulder to make sure that the rest of the world was still following.

Where did it come from, that confidence? Was it his roots? Carter knew who his ancestors were. He knew their names, their stories. His people were rooted in the land. Mine weren't. I once met Carter's father. Carter called him "Sir," and the two greeted each other without touching. He took us to Locke-Obers where the maitre d' saluted him by name, and where he sent an unsuccessful dish back to the kitchen, the apologetic waiters scurrying to put things right.

But maybe you can take the matter of background and roots too far. Life plants the richest seeds in the most unlikely soils at times. A woman like Carter's, for instance. A primrose. What would it matter where she came from or who her parents were? The flower's fragrance draws us in, not the smell of the soil. What would it matter?

It mattered to Carter though. He stopped seeing her, and it troubled me. Even though she never looked at me for two seconds, it troubled me. He had gone to her apartment, and while she was in the bathroom preparing to go out, he stole a look in an envelope lying on a table. Carter told me this himself. It was a letter from her mother, an ordinary letter from home. Nothing shocking or surprising in the thing, but the mother used the language imprecisely. Instead of "really" she wrote "real." *We were real thrilled to hear about the work you've done with those retarded children*, she wrote. Or something like that.

I was real proud of you.

It made Carter's stomach go funny. It changed the way he saw her, changed the way he felt about her. He didn't say anything to her directly—what could he say?—but that was the end of it. He decided not to see her anymore. That's what he told me. He assumed that I would understand.

Carter had other lovers after that, but I didn't know them. He had sensed my disapproval, and a coldness came between us. He tried to explain to me about making fine distinctions, but that embarrassed us. He saw too late that it would embarrass us.

He went on to become a lawyer. His father had been a lawyer. And I heard that he married well. Carter would have to be among the first to note that marrying well isn't at all the same as marrying good. I wish that I knew that he married good as well.

Victoria and Jerry

Victoria and Jerry were strangers who passed each other often on the street. Jerry usually hurried along, lugging a green book-bag over his shoulder. Victoria carried her things in a khaki knapsack and wore long dresses of bright Indian-printed fabrics. She usually took her time, and now and then she stopped to look at the things that interested her: a stray kitten shivering in an alley, an abandoned baby-carriage, the few gaunt trees. Jerry figured her to be a typical Cambridge hippie, right out of *Zap Comix*, someone who sewed her own clothes, ate brown rice, and smoked a lot of dope. Who knows, maybe she could pronounce the names of all those mystics and swamis. Victoria supposed he was a student, a would-be radical perhaps, who lived off a fat allowance and who, at any moment, might shave his beard, cut his hair, and go to law school. As time passed, they started acknowledging each other with their eyes, then by saying hello, and one fine day, Jerry found himself at Victoria's side walking their common way up Inman Street to Broadway.

They learned from each other the sorts of things one shares with strangers. He was a Virgo; she, a Leo. He drew cartoons for the *Rabid Dog* and was planning to go to graduate school in design "at the Museum School or any other place that decides to risk accepting me." She was in her second year of a Women's Studies program, "an off-campus deal, kind of a correspondence course for feminists." She also worked the vitamin counter at Adam's Drug Store in Central Square. He shared a place up on Kirkland Street with two old friends from Harvard and a guy who sold leather belts on Mass. Ave. She lived on Cambridge Street "with six or sometimes seven women, depending."

Victoria said she read the *Rabid Dog* all the time and thought the cartoons were "dreadful, usually." Jerry laughed and said, "Yeah, not every cartoonist lacks that certain something."

Jerry observed that Victoria wore no makeup. Victoria noticed that Jerry bit his nails.

From time to time, over the next few weeks, they walked homeward together. Both complained about the citywide rent hike, but they gloated together over the ever more damning evidence against Nixon. And they argued the merits of cat-owning and dog-owning in a city. Jerry would have a dog if his landlord allowed pets. Victoria's landlord didn't allow pets, but she had cats anyway.

Jerry enjoyed Victoria's irreverent mind. He turned an observation she had made into a cartoon: President Nixon, unshaven and haggard around the jowls, boasting, "As one of my predecessors put it, You *can* fool all of the people some of the time." Victoria was pleased to notice that Jerry really listened. He didn't interrupt her at whim and change the subject, as most men did, and he didn't assume that they would always talk about what was on his mind.

Victoria found Jerry attractive, too. More than attractive: huggable. She wanted to touch his beard with her hand, and she wondered if it was soft. It looked soft. It was funny to think about touching Jerry, though, because men hadn't appealed to her in a long time.

At random moments, Jerry found Victoria attractive, too—when the light struck her in a certain way, when an expression of sudden doubt rearranged her features appealingly. But such moments came and went, and for the most part Jerry would have said, if pressed, that Victoria's looks were "only so-so." But Jerry also would have said, "Looks aren't everything; look at all the fun Henry Kissinger has."

One day Victoria told Jerry about growing up in Hartford. She had lived near Harriet Beecher Stowe's house, in what was Katherine Hepburn's childhood neighborhood as well. Victoria had read half the books in the Mark Twain branch on Farmington Avenue before her library card was revoked because she wouldn't return any of the Virginia Woolf novels. She was thirteen or fourteen and just had to have them. Later, her guidance counselor at Hartford Public had been disappointed because she decided to go to Antioch College instead of Radcliffe or Vassar, schools that had offered her larger scholarships. Victoria's mother was an artist who had to sell encyclopedias door-to-door to make a living.

"What about your father?" asked Jerry.

"Oh, him. My mother dropped him when I was two. He was no prize. A typical man. A bastard. You know the type: nasty, brutish, and short."

"Very funny," said Jerry. "I wasn't crazy about my father either, but in the last couple of years we've started to get along."

"You mean he sends you checks."

"How did you know that?"

Victoria looked down at Jerry's expensive boots and said, "Just a guess."

"Well, there's more to it," said Jerry. "I started to think, when he was my age, when he was twenty-three, I was already born. How can I blame them, I mean my mother, too, for making such a mess of things. In their shoes, I—"

"Are your parents divorced, too?" asked Victoria.

"Many a time and oft." Jerry explained about his mother's four marriages and his father's two. "We moved around a lot."

"Is your mother married now?"

"No, I think she's outgrown it."

"It? You mean marriage or men?"

"Men, I suppose," allowed Jerry.

"But your mother isn't your age now; she isn't twenty-three."

"Of course not. She's in her forties."

"Well, then," said Victoria, "perhaps she's learned something about men that you haven't."

*   *   *

One Friday, Jerry asked Victoria if she ever thought how odd it was that they saw each other only on the street. "Sometimes," he said, "I get the sense that your life is set up with everything in its place. Over here, on Wednesdays, is your women's group. On Thursdays it's the food co-op. On Tuesdays it's yoga. Down here are your house-meetings. Over here are your cats. In this corner—here, on the corner—you make room for me. Walking down the street is where I fit in."

"Oh, come off it, Jerry," replied Victoria. "You know I don't take yoga."

"Well, what do you do on Tuesday nights? Karate? Auto shop? Ceramics?"

"I have co-counseling."

Victoria had always thought that compartmentalizing one's life was something that only men did. She had formed an image of their brains. Sex loomed in the forefront, next to ambition. Love, hunched to the back, was always in danger of being overwhelmed by a tumorous ego. She was annoyed at Jerry's comments, but her reply caught both of them by surprise.

"What about that blonde, preppy-looking woman I saw you with on Saturday at the Café Pamplona?"

"That's Yvonne. She lives in Wellesley."

"Is she your lover?"

"She was. Well, we never really lived together. Really."

"Really?"

"She used to come in on weekends, but the relationship had a lot of problems."

"Problems?" Victoria showed that expression of sudden doubt Jerry liked so well.

"She didn't like my ties," Jerry said, making his voice go funny, "and she complained that my posture was lousy—did you notice that, the way I slouch sometimes?—and she despaired over my table manners, and the way I eat too fast, and my sense of direction—"

"Jerry, why won't you be serious with me?"

Jerry paused and dropped his gesturing hand to his side. Before Victoria could add anything more, he looked at her directly and said, "You know, one of the things I value about our association is that I can say what I feel, whatever it turns out to be."

Victoria was pleased to hear Jerry say that he valued their "association," as he put it. She asked him if there were things he really wanted to say about "that blonde woman." Jerry then told her the story of his affair with Yvonne.

He had met her at a going-away party for the advertising editor of *Rabid Dog*, and he'd been drawn right away to her Colgate smile and healthy blondness. She looked as if she'd just stepped off a tennis court. It turned out she was interested in welfare reform and did legal aid work. She said she loved her work even if it was frustrating and only wished she could "fit two or three more hours into the day."

"Well, you don't have to sleep, do you?" Jerry had said.

Yvonne had looked at Jerry funny, and he had had to explain that he was a cartoonist and his remark had been meant as a joke, a quip. Yvonne had never met a cartoonist before. She apologized, explaining that she had no sense of humor. Jerry reassured her, remarking that people often said the same of him.

After that party, Yvonne had met him for coffee in the Square a few times on weekdays when she could get away from the poor and abused people over in Dorchester. A few times she had had to cancel their plans at the last minute. Once she simply failed to appear at all. Jerry admired such commitment and independence. She didn't put men first—a woman of the future. Jerry did a cartoon sequence about a woman who says, right after making love, "That was nice, kid. Listen, I'll give you a call sometime." That was how he imagined it would be with Yvonne; she would sit up on the edge of the bed untangling her blouse, saying, "I'm sorry, but I really have to run. There's a rent hearing at City Hall I just have to get to."

Jerry continued telling the story to Victoria, even though they had long ago reached the corner where their routes took them in separate directions.

"But once Yvonne and I did start to sleep together, things changed." She began telephoning Jerry's house repeatedly, disturbing Jerry and his housemates. She dropped by unexpectedly and began to neglect the poor. She said she had fallen in love. She said she had to follow her feelings. Her independence vanished. She lost weight. As Jerry put it, "Here was a woman who seemed perfectly capable of fulfilling herself as an individual who, in an instant, right before my eyes practically, melted into a puddle of dependency." What had happened had caught him by surprise. Could his perceptions of Yvonne have been so wrong? The affair had shaken him up. Seeing her again at the Pamplona on Saturday had been difficult. And he had had no one to discuss it with. Not until now.

Victoria remained silent after Jerry finished his story, and Jerry felt reassured. He had pictured her calling him a chauvinist pig or something because he wasn't the one who had ended up in tears. When Victoria did speak, she said, "I can't really picture you with a tennis player."

"She didn't actually play tennis. She just looked like she did."

"You know what I mean."

"I guess so." Jerry felt accepted as a person.

"Let me ask you this, Jerry. Do you *know* what you want from a relationship?"

Jerry lifted both palms in front of him toward Victoria as though pleading for something. "I'd like to be involved with someone who's able to give me enough space for me to be myself."

Victoria tried hard not to wince. She looked around at all the space there was, at the stream of people walking on both sides of Inman Street, all heading away from Mass. Ave., away from the subway and the buses and the hot world of work. She saw a few people walking as couples, but nearly everyone walked alone. People are so isolated, she reminded herself.

"So, what about it?" said Jerry.

"What about what?"

"About getting together sometime besides on the street."

    *   *   *

A week later, Jerry came to dinner at Victoria's house. He offered to help in the kitchen, but as there was nothing he knew how to do, he went into the living room to watch Cronkite with four of Victoria's housemates. Jerry tried to ignore the way the hefty one with braids and an old B.U. sweatshirt refused to acknowledge his presence. He noticed that the place smelled of kitty litter, the green kind. The sofa had bad springs, so he had to sit just right. The liquid in the water pipe was discolored; it looked like tea. From a poster on the wall, the swami Meher Baba advised, "Don't worry. Be happy."

It was hard to be happy. Erlichman or Haldemann—Jerry couldn't keep them straight—was testifying: "I'm sorry, Senator, but to the best of my recollection, I don't recall that." Then one of the plumbers was shown taking the Fifth Amendment. Then Sam Ervin of the Watergate committee was making a statement to reporters. Jerry could never decode his accent. He wished they would use subtitles. Where was he from? Tennessee? Jerry wondered how anyone ever understood a single word the senator said. He pictured a cartoon sequence in which Ervin's remarks were simultaneously translated into incomprehensible Japanese, incomprehensible French, incomprehensible Russian, and so on.

Victoria and her housemates were, it turned out, vegetarian. Dinner was something done to beans. Jerry volunteered to do the dishes. The one with braids handed him the soap. He was careful to do a good job.

Afterward, Victoria and Jerry walked to the Brattle Theater and saw *Memories of Underdevelopment*, the new Cuban film. Victoria thought the hero was still a "sexist pig." Jerry suggested that he was meant to be. "They're trying to tell us that even when you make a revolution, all the bourgeois stuff doesn't suddenly vanish. You can change a label a lot quicker than you can change a person."

"Are you saying that all we have to look forward to are good intentions and new labels and the same old male crap?"

"Well, that and a lot of cartoon ideas, I suppose."

"I don't know, Jerry," said Victoria, stopping suddenly as they walked by the Pewter Pot. "Try telling that to a dead peasant or a raped woman."

$$*\qquad*\qquad*$$

In Jerry's room one could sit on either side of two chairs or on the large and neatly made bed. Jerry took the director's chair while Victoria explored the room.

"Jesus, you have a lot of books."

"One of my mother's husbands worked in a publishing house."

"Did he give you this one?"

"*Sisterhood Is Powerful?* No, that was something Yvonne wanted me to read."

"Any particular reason?"

"To the best of my recollection, I don't recall that."

"Did you read it?"

"Can I plead the Fifth on that?"

Victoria looked at the clothing in Jerry's closet.

"You have a tuxedo! I don't think I've ever known anyone who owned a tuxedo."

"Well," said Jerry, "I used to live in a foreign country: the past."

"Wear it much?" Victoria asked.

"One of these days I'll take it over to the Goodwill."

Jerry had brought Victoria to his room to prove that a man can take a woman home and not even think of pouncing. Victoria had agreed to come because, at the very least, he was attractive, and it had been such a long time.

Victoria sat down on his bed, then drew up her legs underneath. She kicked off her sandals, stared at Jerry, and smiled. Jerry noticed that the soles of her feet were dirty. He and Victoria fell into a silence, and it lengthened.

Jerry knew what it would mean if he were doing what Victoria was doing. He grew uncomfortable and felt pursued. He brought out his photograph album and handed it to Victoria. She leafed thorugh it on the bed, but after a minute asked him to tell her who the people in the photographs were. To do this, Jerry had to join her on the green blanket.

"You certainly know a lot of women," Victoria observed.

"Some of my best friends—"

"Who's this?"

"Someone I used to know."

"Used to know?"

"We broke up. That was a few years ago."

"Are all these women your ex-lovers?"

"Can I plead the Fifth again?"

"Seriously, Jerry."

The room seemed a little hot to Jerry, so he had to open a window.

"A few are just friends," he said. "A few are relatives. This one's my cousin."

"That's fine, Jerry, since she looks like she's about six. How come you have so many ex's?"

"I don't know. I don't have much luck finding women who are strong enough. I intimidate them after a while. This sounds bad, but maybe a good woman is hard to find?"

Soon they ran out of photographs, and after that they ran out of Jerry's cartoon sketches. He showed her his college yearbook and then the model whaling boat he had built in prep school after reading *Moby-Dick*. Victoria smiled, and Jerry tolerated. Jerry bit his nails and grew tense.

Around two o'clock, Victoria performed the coup de grace. "Jerry," she asked, "do you know how to seduce a feminist?"

None of the replies that flashed through Jerry's mind seemed safe to verbalize. "You slip a note inside her copy of *A Room of One's Own*?" "You get another feminist to do it for you?" Jerry didn't know what to say.

It didn't matter. Victoria supplied the answer. "You don't." And then she kissed him.

Victoria's kiss was soft and pleasing, yet Jerry felt an uncomfortable pang of not being in control. Was this what a woman feels when a man makes his move? But when Jerry opened his eyes to that attractive look of doubt on Victoria's face, he felt better. He tried to bury his doubts and feel passionate.

Victoria kissed him again and gently soothed his beard with her palm, something she had long wanted to do. It wasn't soft as she had imagined. She was disappointed. But to Jerry it felt good. He relaxed. He surrendered.

Afterward, Jerry felt dislocated. "That was beautiful," he said. "Are my arms and legs on straight?"

"You don't have to talk," said Victoria, climbing back into her clothes. Jerry wondered how she knew he didn't like to talk afterward.

"That was nice," said Victoria, getting up from the edge of the bed after fastening her sandals. "Listen," she went on, "I'll give you a call sometime."

"Do that," said Jerry. He thought she was making a joke. He had told her about that old cartoon of his, hadn't he? But Victoria walked out the door, and Jerry heard her footsteps on the stairs and then the click of the front door. He wished she had stayed.

Jerry doubted that he would be able to fall asleep after all of that, but he was wrong.

Over the next few days, Jerry telephoned Victoria's number three times. The voice on the other end always sounded like the woman in braids, and she said Victoria wasn't in. He wondered why he hadn't seen her at all on Inman Street. When he finally got her on the phone (by calling Adam's Drug Store), he asked if they could get together that night, but it was Tuesday and she had co-counseling. She said she'd get back to him. She didn't.

She was avoiding him. He didn't understand why. Could it have been the sex? He thought there was a misunderstanding—they could talk!—and tried even harder to pin her down. He left notes in her mailbox, then lengthy letters reexamining all his assumptions and perceptions.

Things bottomed out completely between them. Victoria's housemates were fielding Jerry's phone calls, and eventually he caught on. She had changed her route home from Inman

Street to Prospect. He settled into the opinion that Victoria was just one of those people who couldn't handle intimacy. He submitted a cartoon sequence with a caption reading, "Within the feminist breast lurks the heart of a woman." The drawing was of a female Jekyll-and-Hyde. The editor rejected it.

Victoria had little trouble putting the incident behind her. She thought about answering his notes and letters, and had even imagined how she might phrase her reply. "I hope you'll think of me as a woman who gave you plenty of space to be yourself," read one of them. "Save your tuxedo for law school," went another. In the end she sent him nothing. After a few weeks she stopped feeling angry. She even started to feel a little sad because it seemed he had had possibilities.

One day she caught a glimpse of him walking up ahead of her on Broadway, and she felt an impulse to catch up to him. She didn't know what she would say. What was there to say? But then she noticed the woman walking beside him. She could see him gesturing with his left hand, the way he used to gesture when he had walked with her. She could imagine him explaining later to this other woman, "Oh, her? She was an interesting story, but I'll have to plead the Fifth." Victoria then slowed her pace and lingered before the Clairol signs in the window of the beauty salon next to the Broadway Market. Brunettes, redheads, and blondes. She was relieved, she realized, that Jerry didn't have a photo of her to add to his collection.

My Name Is Buddy

I was once in love with a nurse. She worked the second shift and came home after midnight. She used to wash her white stockings in the bathroom sink and hang them to dry over the shower curtain rod. If she noticed her face in the bathroom mirror, she might have seen the tired mask of a nurse. Upstairs, though, in the darkness of our room, she would slip out of her uniform and mask and find me, and we would drift into the night like sea otters.

On Saturday afternoons, I used to read to her or talk to her for hours. On and on I would drone while she sat on the sofa working a needle through her sewing patterns. One time, I posed some involved question about aesthetics or morality, and she just put her arms around me and said she didn't know why I married her.

She left me. She moved to Vermont and found a job in another hospital. First she lived in the nurses' residence, but soon she moved in with someone named Fred. Or Greg.

That was months ago. Since then, she's driven down to Greenfield to see me once, me and the dog. But the dog had been hit by a truck. "The only thing to do," she said, "is go out and get another."

She stayed for dinner, my version of her recipe for steamed vegetables, with noodles on the side. She complained about land prices in Vermont, saying "We've been to three agents already, and we've traipsed through half the state." The sharp edge of her choice of pronoun cut me out. I was still living the life of the first person singular.

I let her do the talking. Most of Vermont is owned by out-of-state interests, she told me, and everything costs too much. And had she known about the nuke plant in Vernon, she'd never have move up there.

"Too late now," said the silence between us.

She looked at me benignly. It was obvious to me that she was pregnant.

"You know, Buddy, I've always missed having male friends. Maybe you'll be my friend now."

She used to complain that the men she knew always turned into lovers or kept trying to. I remembered how banal she could be.

I asked if she missed me or ever thought about me. She said she missed being involved with someone who had interests in life besides her. This fellow Fred, she went on, had had a drinking problem in the past, before she met him. Now he had her.

"What were my interests besides you?" I asked, wanting to live again in her thoughts.

"Oh, you know, your books, your ideas, your university friends."

I told her that what I missed about her was her love. I said she was the only woman I'd ever known who knew how to show it. I had forgotten how banal I could be. Sugar. Baby. Pussycat.

I walked her out the back door to her car, the same battered, purple Volvo but now bearing shiny green Vermont plates. She got in, rolled down her window, leaned out her elbow, and started to say something. I was just standing there by the driveway, my hand in my hair, looking at her. She opened the door again, walked over, and hugged me. As she got back into the car she said, "Buddy, maybe you have to start taking some risks."

"Like what?" I replied. "Like living next to a nuclear reactor with an ex-wino?"

"No, Buddy. Like having a family and putting down some roots."

Her new friend was ready to make babies and build a little cottage in the woods, unlike me.

She drove off.

Where did that leave me? Where *does* it leave me? Today I

drove around town. Down Wells Street I thought of the dusty old houses, triple deckers, cramped together, elbowing each other. What if one of these old termite-havens collapsed? The dust would stay in the air all day. I'd like to see that, but it won't happen. Those houses have been around for a long time, and gravity isn't moody.

I turned the car onto Pierce Street and saw children doing calisthenics in the schoolyard. They were lined up in rows and were led by a woman in a white uniform.

I also noticed the faces of the drivers in the other lane, looking harmless and bland. Life is ordinary.

Maybe I should go back into therapy. That would put the whole business into perspective. Beth walked out on me and got pregnant by another man . . . and I went back into therapy. Beth got tired of waiting around and decided to leave me and put down some roots . . . and I went back into therapy. Something like that.

What would I say to a therapist? What would I tell him? "I know a teacher at the Day Activities Program, a man who works with some of my retarded clients. He smashed his car into a telephone pole right outside Franklin County Public Hospital."

"Um hmm," I can hear the therapist say. "You have some feelings about this?"

"He doesn't even remember what hit him. The base of the telephone pole was in splinters. The car was wrecked. He woke up in a hospital bed so fractured he couldn't talk about it. He couldn't piece it together."

"I see," the therapist would say. "But perhaps there is something that you can't piece together."

I have a friend who is a therapist. He is not my therapist, but he would like to be. He would like me to *confront my feelings*. He says that anyone whose wife has left him and gets pregnant by another man has got to have some pretty strong feelings about it.

"If you're looking for work," I tell him, "I've got a nice, screwed-over quadriplegic on my caseload who watches television all day. He needs counseling. For starters, there's the messy business of his sexuality."

This usually stalemates us. I don't want to make pictures in my head of Beth getting pregnant with somebody named Fred or Greg, and he doesn't want to make pictures in his head of my quadriplegic on his couch.

My therapist-friend's name is Lehmann. The teacher at the Day Activities Program's name is Michael Baugham. Beth's name is Beth. My name is Buddy. Life is ordinary. The quadriplegic's name is Arthur.

Maybe I'll forget about therapy and put the matter to Arthur. That would place the whole business in perspective, too. Beth walked out and got pregnant, and I talked it over with Arthur, my retarded, quadriplegic client who has sat in front of a television set for six years.

Arthur would say, "I don't think you should have let her go. You should have married her."

"I did marry her. It didn't help."

Arthur's two hands are glued in front of his chest like the little paws of a squirrel stiffened by rigor mortis. But his neck muscles are bullish, and he can swivel his head around. I picture Arthur in his wheelchair, swiveling his head toward me to answer.

"You love her, don't you?"

"Right. Right. But it's too late. She's pregnant by another man and worries about nuclear reactors and land prices. She even wants me to be her friend. There's no going back. What should I do?"

Well, Arthur, what about that?

"The only thing to do," he'd say, "is to go out and get another."

Because he's been watching television so much, Arthur knows all the angles when it comes to ordinary stuff, ordinary lives. Arthur could picture television solutions to my problems.

Beth miscarries and blames this guy Fred. Or maybe the nuclear reactor. And she gets lonely for my books and my fancy ideas and my university friends. She comes back and, like sea otters in the night, we slip away and make babies and build cottages in the woods.

Or, suddenly I wake up in Intensive Care and don't remember a thing. I was riding my car down Wells Street when one of those triple-decker houses flopped onto my car, swirling dust, obliviousness. A nurse is peering down with loving eyes, saying, "Don't try to talk. Everything's going to be all right."

Come on, Arthur, one more.

I am driving down Pierce Street, preoccupied with my inability to take risks, when a child dashes in front of the car. His schoolmates stop exercising and begin to scream. If I hit him and he isn't killed, will he become a quadriplegic? Will I be his caseworker? I swerve to avoid him, the brakes squealing. The car hits a hydrant instead. The school nurse has run to my car door, breathless, and we . . .

On and on and on. So now I've got daydreams about Arthur having my own fantasies for me. And Beth's up in Vermont, lost for good. The dog's been dead for over a month. And I'm going to be thirty soon.

Maybe I should get another dog and teach him to sit up and take some risks. We could drive together in the car, up Wells Street, down Pierce Street, and the drivers in the other lane could look over and see us, a young man and his dog, driving along, harmless and bland, avoiding all the falling houses and telephone poles.

October Reeds

I used to send personal notices to my college's alumni magazine, but I don't bother anymore. I stay at home all day and do next to nothing. Today I am standing at the sink, thinking about finding a job, when a stranger walks in through the unlatched screened door of this farmhouse we rent, Ruthie and I. He says he's the plumber. But he doesn't look like a plumber. He looks like Robert Redford playing a young and cagey plumber who is really working undercover. I wonder why he's come, as Ruthie hadn't mentioned calling a plumber.

"Your pump is broken, isn't it?" he asks.

"I don't think so."

"You got running water?"

"Take a look at this!" I hand him a breakfast plate, newly rinsed and dried.

"I don't see my reflection."

"That wasn't my point."

"Listen, Bronsky called this morning and asked us to fix the pump out here."

"Bronsky? I thought he was in mourning?"

"Does it matter? Look, he's paying, so what's it to you?"

I point out the stairs to the basement, but he says if it's okay with me he'll go through the cellar doors outside. He says his truck and equipment are out by the cellar doors. Those cellar doors are like the ones Auntie Em closes when the twister hits in *The Wizard of Oz*.

Because the water is turned off, I stop doing dishes. I start typing cover letters. The plumber doesn't know what I'm typing. Maybe he thinks I'm writing something important—a book about undulant fever or atmospheric inversions—and that's why I'm at home in the middle of the day. It wouldn't occur to him that I'm an ex-philosophy graduate student whose committee had reluctantly (so it says) flunked him during his orals for "failing to abide by the simple canons of rational thought and conventional scholarly discourse." At least today I've shaved.

I become accustomed to the sound of metal on metal down in the basement. At desultory intervals, he seems to be striking at something. I type two letters and begin a third. Then he stops. I wait for him to begin again, but he doesn't, and in a moment I see through the window that he's back at his truck.

He disappears from sight, but in a minute I hear him climbing the inside stairs to the kitchen. What now?

"Is it all right if I use your phone?" he yells.

He dials and hangs up the receiver, then redials and again hangs up the receiver. Is he getting a busy signal or sending a coded message? I hear his footsteps descending. I try framing sentences in my head: *And although I have not actually had any previous experience teaching math to disturbed adolescents . . .* I hear nothing from the basement. Great silences invade the pauses between my words.

I hear him climbing the stairs once more. Again he dials. Again he hangs up the phone. He stays in the kitchen. I sense him there, waiting, and lose my concentration. I switch off the typewriter and go into the kitchen to speak to him.

"Almost finished?"

"Nope. Not getting anywhere. I've got to call in."

"Maybe you could look at the bathroom sink. It's been leaking ever since we rented this place."

"The sink or the faucet?"

"The faucet."

"Bronsky want it fixed?"

"I don't know, but that faucet really is broken."

"It's up to Bronsky."

"Oh. Well, there's something else. Our electric water heater is on too high. Can we do anything about that?"

"You mean it's too hot?"

"We don't want to waste electricity."

"Yeah, that could eat up a lot of juice."

We climb down to the basement together. Ruthie's paintings are hanging all over the place. I try to see through the plumber's eyes. He's in a country house where they have big, crazy paintings in the cellar and there's this guy who sits around typing all day, this guy who knows nothing about how things work.

Getting at the water heater is hard because Ruthie's big easels are in the way.

"Look," he says, "it's really simple. You just unscrew this panel, and see this dial here? Just push it over a little to the left, see."

He bends out of sight. I bend, too, and notice a lunar surface of dust on the back of the water heater.

"There," he says, "I've set it to a hundred-thirty. See?"

"Yes," I lie.

"There's another panel down here that has to be unscrewed. It's a thermostat system. Both the top and the bottom have to agree."

"Thanks a lot. Really," I say and start wondering what happens if the top and bottom don't agree.

"You can come down here and readjust it yourself. Just watch out you don't catch any juice."

"Okay."

"I'm not supposed to be doing this stuff, by the way, so don't mention it, all right?"

We return to the kitchen, and he tries his call again. No luck.

"Would you like a beer?" I ask.

"No thanks," he says, "I still have a couple of stops to make. Thanks anyway."

I don't have any stops to make, so I open a can. I don't know what to say next, so I say nothing.

"Who died?" he asks.

"Bronsky's kid brother."

"Yeah?"

"He was only forty or so."

"Yeah?"

"He was over here just the other week when that carpet over there was starting to smell like cabbage. He certainly seemed

alive then. He told me he grew up in this house; all the brothers did. Their old man planted those maples outside. The
brothers put in the sumac and those reeds."

"What was it? A stroke?"

"Heart attack. With some kind of complications. I think he
drank a lot."

"Was he into real estate, too?"

"Just the rug business and those U-Hauls. Only Bronsky
does real estate."

"Any kids?"

"He wasn't even married."

"Funny."

"They say he almost did once. Get married. There's a story
about him and some local woman who was a little bonkers.
The families broke it up. She left or was put somewhere—
something like that."

He tries his call again and gets through. He is talking, and I
return to my typewriter. Maybe he wants to invite a plumber
buddy to share the work on Bronsky's pump. I begin typing
envelopes and once again hear metal clanking from the
basement.

Then I sense someone behind me and turn around. Another stranger. One of these days, I think, I'll fix the latch on
that door. This man doesn't look like a plumber either.

"Oh. I'm sorry to just walk in like this. I did knock."

"That's okay. It's downstairs."

I return to my envelopes, but he doesn't move.

"Maybe you can help me," he says. "Do you plant those
things growing out back?"

"You're not with the plumbers?"

"Plumbers? No, I'm with the cub scouts. Our pack is making fall decorations. Do you have any idea how expensive
those things are in the stands? They charge two dollars for a
bunch of those."

"Those reeds?"

"I was wondering if I could take a few . . . for the pack."

"I was a cub scout."

"It's for Pack 375. In Greenfield."

"Well, we only rent this place. They really belong to the landlord. You know Bronsky?"

"Bronsky?"

"How many do you need, anyway?"

"Maybe a dozen?"

"Oh, if that's all, you might as well just take them. I'll get you some scissors."

"That's all right. I can just tear them off."

"It's easier with scissors."

I bring the scissors, then decide to walk outside with him. I see a woman waiting in a car in front of the house. The man calls out to her. "It's all right!"

Her reply is undecipherable.

"It's all right!" he repeats. "Come on!"

The woman crosses the lawn. There's a little girl, too, maybe four or five years old. The child is very genial and says "Hi" just like Lauren Bacall. "Hi."

The woman is awkward and averts her eyes. She says nothing. She looks older than her husband, if he is her husband. She also looks like she is still living in the 1940s. She wears a kerchief and her glasses have sequins in the frames. Another imposter? Is she after Robert Redford the plumber or is he after her?

The man asks the woman to pick out which reeds, but she just stands there. The little girl skips across the lawn. The man cuts down seven or eight of the wispy reeds. I stand by, and no one says anything. The wind scrapes fallen leaves across the driveway, past the plumber's truck. I break off a reed and hand it like a balloon to the little girl.

"What's you name, sweetheart?" I ask her.

"My mom has a friend, and he lives in heaven!"

"Oh? And did he find you there and give you to her?"

"Yes! No!"

The man is hurrying to finish. The woman's vacant gaze is disturbed when the child tries to tickle her face with the reed.

"Please, honey!"

I watch them return to their car. I call out, "Good luck with the pack!"

"Yeah, sure, and thanks!" says the man. The woman looks back at me vacantly.

I turn and face the hills on the horizon. Winter's not far off, at least that's certain. The air is cool. The reeds appear as a delicate frost across the lines of the blazing sumacs. The grass is straw in the fields. The wind scrapes more leaves across the driveway. I start to think the leaves are like erasers dragging across a page.

When I return to the house, I forget the plumber is here. It occurs to me that were I still a graduate student, I'd be on campus now, sitting in a room without windows. But I am not a graduate student, and I let the novel I've been reading put me in a Minnesota prairie town around the turn of the century. I spend some time there—maybe an hour. Maybe two.

Then the plumber comes up to report. From where he stands he cannot see what I'm reading, so he probably thinks it's important and related to my work on undulant fever.

"I couldn't get it fixed today. I'll come back when I get parts."

"How long will that take?"

"Beats me. Maybe a week. I turned the water back on. You can still use it."

"Okay."

"Did you see Bronsky?" he asks.

"Today?"

"He came down through the cellar doors. In black. He wasn't very pleased."

"I'll bet."

"Well, I'll see you."

"Oh, thanks again for the water heater."

"Don't mention it."

"I won't."

The plumber leaves, and I return to the novel. Evening's coming on. I see Ruthie's car pull into the driveway. She marches into the house and says, "Shit!" and then goes to the sink with the milk jar in her hands.

"The milk leaked all over the car. I put the brakes on and the jar tipped over, damn it!"

"That's a shame."

"How would you like to drive to the dairy and get some more?"

"The plumber came today. He couldn't fix the pump."

"What's wrong with the pump?"

"Nothing, as far as I can tell."

"Well, why did he come?"

"Bronsky sent him."

"Why is Bronsky worrying about the pump?"

"His brother died of a heart attack."

"Yes, the brother. I stopped when I saw the burial going on."

"The burial?"

"At that old graveyard on River Road."

"A lot of people there?" I ask.

"Not so many," says Ruthie. "People from town, a few strangers."

"Strangers?"

"Yeah, like this one lady with sequins in her glasses. Frumpy-looking, even for around here."

"Was she with a little kid and a man?" I ask.

"Couldn't say. She stood out because she caused a little scene. She kept trying to drop some flowers or something into the grave, and Bronsky stopped her, and she was crying."

"You didn't see any cub scouts?"

"At a burial?"

"It's a long story."

"Another long story! Sometimes I think I understand how you managed to screw up your orals."

"Come on, Ruthie. Maybe if my committee spent some time out here they'd . . ."

"Sure, sure! I can just hear you: 'There are more things in heaven and earth, Professor Pietzsche, than are dreamt of in your philosophy.'"

"I think I'll get the milk now," I say, and turn to go.

"Oh, hell!" says Ruthie.

"What now?"

"I think the pump really is broken."

"What?"

"I turned on the faucet to rinse the jar, but I don't see any water. Do you?"